MORNING STAR RISES

Doorway Series
Book II

Merrilyn Grove

ISBN 978-0-615-14525-9

The Doorway Series:
Mockingbird Sings
Morning Star Rises
Jaguar Speaks

Childrens' Books
Angel and the Magic Granny
I Don't Want a Haircut

Other works
Daughter of the Seventh Son: A MoonBeam
Mystery (Co-Authored with Betty Kidwiler)

DEDICATED to my life teachers:

To my father, Joseph Grove: You taught me to care about others and about the state of the world, for which I am forever grateful.

To my brothers, Mel and John: You are my best friends, and have given me two wonderful sisters in the form of your wives, Audrey and Louise.

Special thanks go to two people, without whom this book would have been much less than it is:

Dolores Voorhees, who volunteered to copyedit my rough manuscript.

Steph Lovik, my computer technician

PROLOGUE

Eyes wide with fear, Star thrashed upon her pallet. Only moments before, she had said goodbye to the people—but in the dream, she was not a woman. She was the man, Quetzalcoatl—come from far away with his group of helpers, to speed the advancement of the people.

Vague glimpses of half-remembered images became full and complete as memories flooded her mind and body, drowning out present time. Quetzalcoatl was one with the brotherhood. Neither male nor female, but with an ethereal body capable of being instantly in more than one place, this consciousness was both individual and a part of the greater group mind. They had been watching over the inhabitants of Earth, waiting for the correct time to make contact while infusing certain evolved ones of Earth with ideas of ways to advance their society. The critical point had been reached, and it was time to go in person—time to make physical contact with these people.

Quetzalcoatl sat high on the mountain, looking down at the beautiful city among the trees of the forest. He had come far from his home, taking on a human body fraught with heaviness and complications. He had done this to help the people of this world—this lush and green paradise world. He had grown to love it; but was, at the same time, eager to leave. He had come to teach the primitive people of Earth, to help them out of the darkness and to bring them into the Light of Love and Truth. They had been good students, eager to learn and to apply all the knowledge he had shared. To them, in their naiveté, he was a god. They gave him the name of "Feathered Serpent" because of the wisdom he imparted. He stayed for years in one land after another, teaching them the basics of agriculture, metalwork, astronomy, and mathematics. He taught them music, dance, scribing, and the arts. When they were able to live without the constant struggle for survival, he took the leaders through the initiatory teachings of the law of the One, which they swore they would teach to the people. Believing he had done all he could at the time, he prepared to leave. He went to the high mountain to commune with his brethren in the home world.

As he sat in communion, he saw the future of this race and he knew they would fall from the ways. The priesthood would not share the teachings with the people as they had promised. Their egos were strong, and they desired power over the others. They would twist and subvert the teachings, and death would come to the land. He felt sick to know he had been an instrument in this perversion, but it was too late to change what was done.

Joining with his brothers, he knew what he must do. He made a pact to come back at a future time in the female form. He would return to finish what he had started. He would be called the Morning Star. As a woman, Morning Star would join forces with another woman called Mockingbird whose previous lives had all been lived on this Earth. Together, they would overcome great difficulties of birth and time to become known as the Enlightened Leaders. They would take the people into the knowledge of the One and the Light. He sat on the mountain and wrote the prophecy onto the bark that he had carried with him.

THE PROPHECY

A great city becomes dark.
The people cry aloud and in silence.
A great heaviness weighs;
All hope is gone.

Blood flows from on high,
Broken bodies fall from the sky,
Fear reigns;
All hope is gone.

Out of the mountain of death
Come two.
Out of the mountain of death,
Hope is reborn.

Both carry the sign:
One with blue eyes,
One with star on brow,
Joining heaven and earth.

Mother Earth swallows,
She spits them out.
She gives new life;
Hope is reborn.

Fragile bodies
Strengthened in trial;
Strong spirits
Become obsidian.

A hidden city
Gives up its secrets.
The door is opened
Between heaven and earth.

One and two
Come to destroy,
Bringing the darkness
To no avail.

Darkness fights Light.
Which will win?
The answer lies within.
Hope lives on.

PART ONE

When he reached the holy sea
and the shore of the luminous ocean,
He stayed his steps and wept.
He gathered his garments together
and dressed himself again
in his robes of quetzal feathers
And his turquoise mask.[1]

1

Star's heart held the sweet ache of mother's love as she smoothed the thick black hair on her baby's head. Looking at her son, so much like his father, she couldn't believe it was possible to love someone so much. This small person gurgled, his breath warm with the smell of her milk, his tiny body soft against her breast, as he reached out to grasp her hair with a strength that surprised her. The infant looked up at her, his eyes staring into hers as if searching deep inside her soul. He seemed to be trying to communicate his happiness at being with her.

Vague stirrings of strange dreams during childbirth nagged at her. She tried to remain still, to recapture the full dream. She knew this was a true dream—a memory of what had gone before. She could see herself as a man. Looking down at her feet, she saw pale skin below the long robe that was edged with embroidered crosses. She clearly saw the hair on the legs, the criss-crossed straps of the sandals, the large feet. The hair falling over the shoulder was a light color, and wavy. She knew the feel of the face as her hand brushed the hair of the chin. The memories became clearer and clearer as she lay there, awed with the knowledge as the details crystallized for her. Her old priestess, long since passed from the earth, had told her she was Quetzalcoatl reborn—and now she remembered. Her memory expanded as she saw and felt the beauty of the union she had with the ones of her home planet. As the veil lifted from her perception, she fully knew her mission—the promise she had made to help Mockingbird bring the people into the Light.

As she filled her eyes with her new son's beauty, the songs of Singer, her nursery caregiver in the Aztec temple, came back to her. She began to hum, and then, to sing the words to him. The song was the Prophecy of the Great Quetzalcoatl, spread far and wide by all of the Singers—the tradition bearers and story tellers. The song had always given her a feeling of mixed melancholy and joy; and now she knew why. It was the song that she had written when in the bodily form of Quetzalcoatl. It told of his work to bring the Light, his knowledge that he had failed, and his intention to return to earth to try again.

Star smiled at her husband as he entered the calli where she had just given birth. She loved this steadfast man. He wasn't the most handsome man in the City, but she didn't see that—she saw only the beauty of his spirit. She gazed at him, now, and saw a bright light emanating from him—surrounding his body, and encompassing everything within the calli. She could feel the love he felt for her. It held a strength and force that could have been overwhelming to a lesser woman. Star knew without the slightest doubt that he would gladly die for her, but that he chose to live for her—to be a steady rock to hold onto in times of doubt, warm arms to comfort in times of need, and joyous playfulness to amuse and delight in times of happiness. He knew the importance of laughter, but he didn't think about it in that way—he didn't force it. It just came naturally to his childlike being.

He knelt beside Star and his new son. "Are you well, my wife?"

"Very well, Husband," Star replied. "Our son gives me no trouble. His birth was easy and he eats well!"

She winced at the tug of her hair in the chubby little fist, and said wryly, "Perhaps I spoke too swiftly!"

Her husband gently disentangled the infant's hand from Star's hair. At the first touch of his newborn son, his heart filled with an urgency that he couldn't name. It was as if he had planned to do something, but the plan escaped his memory. The memory tugged at his mind, but he couldn't draw it forth. He had more and more of these "tugs" since the jumping snake had bitten him and he had gone to the other side of death and back.

It had happened when he had been among those who followed Mockingbird and Star from the Aztec capitol of Tenochtitlan through the jungles, over the mountains, and through the very bowels of the Earth to the New City. Star had been on the brink of womanhood then, and he had loved her from the first time he saw her. He knew she was destined to become a Great Seer and Priestess of the One, while he was a mere mortal and an ex-slave. He was content to worship her from his place in life, but then a miracle happened. While standing guard one night, a jumping snake bit him, poisoning him and taking him into the underworld. He had died for a brief time, and while his spirit was parted from his still body, he understood many things. He met a Spirit of Light, which told him who he really was. He was much more than an ex-slave from Tula. When he recovered, the Priestesses Tlacotl and Morning Star gave him a new name. From that time forward, he bore the honorable name of Jumping Snake. It had been revealed that he was gifted with wisdom and had a willingness to change his life. He had strong powers of intuition and the ability to travel in spirit. He could leave his body at rest while his spirit traveled to far places. He was gifted with Snake Medicine.

Now, Snake smiled widely as Star placed their child in his hands. He held the boy with great tenderness—afraid his hands might be too rough.

Star, so sensitive to the feelings of others, said, "He is fine, is he not? And strong, so you needn't fear holding him!"

Snake answered, "He is the finest of sons, my wife! Do you know his name?"

With a mischievous smile, she said, "I don't know his name but you know him well, my husband. At the Naming Ceremony, you will tell us who he is."

The memory once again tugged at Snake's mind, but it still eluded him. He said, "My Wife, I feel that I know him, but I cannot bring the memory forth. When I look upon his infant body, he is my beloved son; but when I look into his knowing eyes, it is as if he is someone else that I should remember."

"It will come to you, my husband—when the time is right!"

At the sound of approaching women, Snake carefully handed the baby back to his wife. "The Queen has been patiently waiting to see how you fare," he said. He brushed the straying hair from his wife's forehead and kissed the star-shaped scar above her brows. Star's heart overflowed with tenderness. The first kiss he ever gave her was on her forehead, and it was his way of telling her that he was always aware of how special she was, and how much he appreciated her.

As her husband left the calli, she could hear him talking outside. "Oh, yes, My Queen. Morning Star is doing well, and our son is very healthy! She is awaiting you, Lady."

"Thank you, Brother," the Queen replied. "I will see her alone."

Mockingbird, the Queen of Ihuicatl—The City of the Door—swooped regally into the calli. Her face lit up as all the cares of leadership dissolved at the sight of her beloved sister and her sister's new son.

"Oh, Little Sister, he is beautiful!" Mockingbird's smile lit her face with joy as she gazed upon Star's infant. She held out her hands to receive the sturdy little body.

Mockingbird sat on a bench, placed the infant on her lap, and removed the swaddling cloth that kept him secure. Looking him over carefully, she finally wrapped him up again and said, "Sister, he is perfect! He does look like his father, doesn't he? Thick hair...wide mouth and large eyes...even to the shape of his toes and fingers...he is like your husband, Snake!" She smiled gently at the child, and then shifted her gaze to Star.

"And you, Sister? You look well! Come. Sit. You shouldn't be standing for a while yet." Mockingbird patted the bench next to her and handed the infant back to Star.

A small child's voice called from outside the door, "Nantli...Auntie...may I come in?"

Mockingbird glanced for approval from Star and then called out, "Enter Daughter!"

Three-year-old Feather was wide-eyed with curiosity as she came through the doorway. She remembered to make a perfunctory bow and greeting to her mother and auntie, pausing for only a second before she darted over to them to peer at the infant.

She stood quietly and stared into the eyes of the baby. Reaching out a hand, she gently touched the small boy on the face. The infant gurgled and fought the restraining cloth.

"Oh, he knows me!" Feather looked up excitedly at her mother and auntie. "May I hold him?"

Star answered, "For a moment, Little One. Sit on the bed and I will put him in your arms."

Feather did as she was bid, and a moment later she held the infant in her small arms and declared, "He is my brother! Oh, I will always take care of him!"

The women smiled at each other, happy that their children would carry on the special bond they had with each other.

They both watched the child and infant while the pictures of their lives poured through their memories. These children—their children—were born into a society their mothers had helped to create. These children would never know the uncertainty and fear they had known.

The New City of Ihuicatl was indeed a door—a door to all that can be. Based on the tenets of the Law of the One, it was a city of love and respect for life. No sacrifice of human beings was demanded in this great city. The laws, handed down from Quetzalcoatl, the Great Prophet, were the guiding forces. Schools, libraries, and medical care were free to the inhabitants of Ihuicatl, as well as to any neighboring people who agreed to live in peace and harmony.

When Mockingbird and Star reached the New City, they immediately recognized that it was the place they had been searching for. It was a huge sprawling city with temples that reached beyond the highest trees of the rain forest. Everything—temples, palaces, houses, plaza, granaries, and courtyards—were overgrown and almost hidden from view by the lush plant life. Not a person walked the streets, but life abounded. Hundreds of brilliantly colored birds sang out their calls to the newcomers. The air was filled with roars from the howler monkeys as they threw fruits at the people, while the smaller spider monkeys chattered loudly as they leaped and swung from branch to branch over their heads. Cougars, jaguars, ocelots, and tapirs moved along the deserted paths and empty causeways. Butterflies and moths filled the air, drawn by the intoxicating fragrance of the myriad of tropical flowers. It was the Door between Heaven and Earth—one of the most powerful spots on Earth. And yet—it was empty of human inhabitants. It was as if it had been built and left to await Mockingbird, Star, and their followers. The animal life seemed to recognize and welcome them as if they, too, knew of the prophecy of the Enlightened Leaders who were to come here.

It had taken three years for the main part of the city to become populated and functioning as they intended. The outlying areas were still as they had found them. Much of the housing surrounding the City center was still uninhabited. Their biggest task had been to pull the city from the arms of the encroaching jungle. Vines and other plant life had swallowed it, almost hiding the enormous buildings from view.

It was a good time for the young Queen Mockingbird and her husband, Eagle. Their daughter, Feather, had been born on the journey, and this city was all that the child remembered. Star, the Priestess of the One, married her husband, Snake, a year later. By that time, with the help of the other friends from the journey, as well as many local people who had been waiting for the Prophecy to be fulfilled, the main buildings and temples had been freed of the jungle growth. The buildings sparkled in the sun, the fountains flowed, and the plaza bustled with activity. The larger animals stayed in the surrounding forest, but the monkeys, birds, and butterflies still inhabited the city along with the people.

To the band of travelers who had made Ihuicatl their home, it was paradise. They had come from a beautiful city, but it had been a city ruled by fear. The Priesthood ruled, even holding sway over the King. They insisted that the gods needed human blood—human energy—as a sacrifice on a regular basis. It was, Star knew, an error in the interpretation of the sacred texts. The ceremonial sacrifices kept the inhabitants of the city and the surrounding territories in a constant state of stress.

If it hadn't been for the wonderful friends and new family who helped them to escape, she and Mockingbird would have been sacrificed to the god Tezcatlipoca. It had been so close. On the eve of the sacrificial ceremony, the Priestess Tlacotl, the nurse Singer, and their brave soldiers had gotten them out of the city and on the road to freedom and a new life. Tlacotl and Singer had died along the way, gladly sacrificing their lives for the promise of a prophecy fulfilled.

As Star watched little Feather holding the baby boy, she knew without a doubt that these two children had been with them before in another lifetime. She could see the greatness in them that was hidden from ordinary eyes. She remembered them from times past, when she had been on earth long ago.

Star said, "Sister, I must tell you what happened to me as I gave birth to my son!"

Mockingbird asked, "What is it, little Sister?"

"I have seen the past, the present, and the future."

2

Jaguar held his breath as the deer browsed in the forest only a few steps from him. There were three of them—a doe and two fawns. Soundlessly, he raised his bow and stood with the arrow drawn. He would surprise his father and mother with fresh deer meat! He had never killed an animal and the other boys had started teasing him, saying that his father—a great soldier—would be ashamed to have a son who couldn't hunt. A movement caught his eye in the trees above the deer. There, hidden among the greenery, was a large cougar, ready to pounce. Instinctively, Jaguar raised his sight to the cougar and let the arrow fly. The cougar dropped to the ground as the doe turned tail and disappeared, followed into the forest by the two fawns.

The cougar didn't move. Jaguar could see the arrow protruding from its heart, and he felt a sick sadness he couldn't understand. It was a beautiful cat, a huge female, tawny and magnificent.

As he stood over the large animal, he remembered how a jaguar had pulled him from the mineral pool when he was a small child. It had sensed danger and taken him to safety. Now, somehow, he was seeing the figure of the spotted jaguar overlying the still body of the golden cougar he had just shot. He turned away as his stomach lurched. After a moment, he again turned to the cougar. Praying to the One for help, he gently removed the arrow. Laying his hands on the wound, he pictured the cat alive and healthy as warmth flowed through his hands. Jaguar suddenly felt the animal move slightly. He held very still, envisioning light entering the animal from his hands. Suddenly, the cougar leaped to its feet and shot away through the forest. Jaguar, tears streaming from his eyes, sat on the ground and trembled.

***

Flower watched for her son. She and her husband, Deer, had hoped to have more children, but she had not become pregnant after Jaguar was born. Still, she didn't feel as if she was missing anything. Jaguar was eight years old. He still resembled his father. His black hair was coarse like Deer's hair and his body was strong. His eyes, alone, were different. Deer had soft brown eyes like the animal he was named for, gentle and kind. Jaguar's eyes had green specks mixed in with the brown. They were very unusual in color, and slanted slightly upward.

Flower noticed that Jaguar seemed to be thinking deeply about something. He usually smiled and chattered when he came back from the forest. He would tell her long stories about the animals he had seen, giving exquisite details about their habits, and sometimes he told her what they seemed to be thinking. It no longer seemed odd to Flower that her son appeared to be able to communicate with animals. She remembered how, on the journey, her little boy had wandered into a deep pool by himself and had been carried to shore by a wild jaguar. She panicked, thinking he had been maimed or killed by the animal. When they discovered he was safe, she realized that her son had a special gift. The Priestess had given him the name of the animal that adopted him, and said she had a vision of the boy's future. He was destined to become a great Shaman!

Ever since that day, Flower and Deer tried to give him as much freedom as possible so he could develop his talent, but they still worried about their only son. Both Flower and Deer had heard whispers and laughter from some of the local children about Jaguar being different. Flower was concerned that her son was being singled out and not being accepted by the other children. Mockingbird and Eagle's daughter, Feather, idolized Jaguar and followed him about; but she was so much younger than the boy, that it caused even more teasing. Jaguar seemed not to notice or care, but Flower wondered secretly if it was possible that the teasing didn't bother him. Now, Flower saw him approaching and thought that he looked distracted.

"Son, come tell me what you have been doing this morning!"

Jaguar's eyes lit up when he saw his mother's gentle face and he walked faster. Bow in hand and arrow quiver slung over one shoulder, he appeared excited as he neared his mother.

He said, "Nantli, something happened today that I must tell you about!"

"Come, Son. Sit and drink while we talk." Flower handed Jaguar a cup of papaya juice from the bench beside her.

He emptied the cup in two swallows, took a deep breath, and he told her what had happened with the cougar.

"Son," Flower said softly. "We must go to see the Priestess, Morning Star—oh, she has just given birth—but, we will talk to her consort, Jumping Snake, instead. He is powerful in the knowledge of the Great One. He will know what to do. It was Morning Star who told me that you would be a great Shaman one day, and her husband knows this. Bathe yourself, Jaguar. Dress in your new clothing and red sandals. I will send a message to the Shaman, to let him know we wish an audience with him."

***

Snake waited for the visit from Flower and Jaguar. He knew that Deer was on a mission for the Queen, and he was surprised that Flower would come to him without her husband present. The families that had begun the journey together were still very close, though they had various types of work to do. Still, Flower retained the shyness and modesty that she had in her youth. Snake knew that she must have something very important to discuss with him, or she would have waited for Deer's return.

As he waited for the woman and boy, he reclined on a couch in his private room and closed his eyes for a moment. Memories flooded through his mind of the long journey he had undertaken with his friends.

It had been an experience filled with dangers and discoveries. It had started for him well before the journey began, when he had been an unassuming pottery maker in the city of Tula. He was married to a young woman he had known all his life. He was in the market place when the soldiers from Tenochtitlan took many prisoners for not paying their dues to the Aztec Empire.

Somehow he and his captor had been separated from the rest of the soldiers and captives on the trip back to the Aztec capitol. Snake (who was then known as Rabbit), was a follower of the Great Quetzalcoatl, the prophet and teacher of old, who came to teach the People the truths and laws of the One Great God in Two Forms, both masculine and feminine. As the soldier and the potter traveled, they began to talk. The soldier, Deer, was curious about why the man from Tula didn't resist when he was captured. Snake explained his beliefs in non-violence. One thing lead to another, and eventually, Snake told Deer that Quetzalcoatl had taught the People to love one another—and to Snake, this meant he was unable to take the life of another man. He said it was an individual interpretation, but it was his belief. By the time the two got back to Tenochtitlan, the two men had become friends. The soldier respected and admired the potter. He tried to set him free, but Snake believed he had been captured by this man for a reason. He refused his freedom. The soldier, Deer, appealed to his superiors to be allowed to keep the Tula man as a household slave. The request was granted, and Snake served in Deer's household for three years before they escaped the city and began the great journey.

A deep sadness filled Snake when he learned his young wife had died in Tula; but his beliefs allowed him to move through the grieving process and celebrate the knowledge that she was in a far happier state of being than she had been in life. He continued to do the work of the household and had come to the point where he felt as if they were his family. He loved Deer, Flower and their small son. Flower was very modest and shy, but she treated him as a brother and the little boy learned to call him Uncle. Deer gave Snake his freedom after the three years were up, but he still lived with the family and taught them all he knew of the Great Quetzalcoatl and the One God.

One day, Deer came to Snake and told him about the two girls who had been given to the Temple on the same day as Flower. Flower had been sent home but the other two had remained. The girls had been taught the mysteries, and had been kept apart and secluded from the world to ensure their purity. They were taught the most advanced knowledge and endured strict physical training. They were trained in the arts—singing, dancing, and musical instruments. Then, at the peak of womanhood, they would be allowed to give up their life force to the gods. The two girls would be sacrificed in a ceremony at the top of the Temple stairs. They were told it was a great honor to be chosen—it meant that they were the best the Empire had to offer. To offer less than perfection would be an affront to the gods who would then take action against the People.

Snake remembered the first time he saw the two whose destiny it was to become the Enlightened Rulers. He remembered the Prophecy about two young women who would bring the People back to the ways and laws of the One. He was stunned when he saw how young and naïve they seemed. Mockingbird, the future Queen, had barely become a woman. But, she had the startling blue eyes prophesized by the Seers. And Star! Snake was immediately captivated by this young woman. She was so pretty; and something about her spoke to his soul. The star-shaped scar on her forehead proved she was the Priestess of the One God. It had been given to her as a sign of her destiny.

Snake had fallen in love with Star—a pure soul love—but she would be a High Seer and he was a mere potter and ex-slave. He was raised in a culture of castes, and he knew his place. Still, he was attracted to her. During the journey, she danced for ceremony. The beat of the drum, her nubile movements, and the heady drink raised a surge of lust in him. He had to leave and go into the forest because he wasn't sure he could control himself. He wanted to ask her to wed him, but she was still too young and he thought she was out of his reach. He chastised himself for his foolishness, and his lack of control.

Snake's memories were interrupted by a server who announced his guests. As Flower and Jaguar entered the room, they lowered their eyes and greeted him. Both were dressed in formal clothing—Flower in a lovely blue shift with an embroidered belt, and Jaguar in a short boy's skirt of the same material. Both mother and son wore sandals with red straps crisscrossed up the calves of their legs.

Snake, happy to see his old friends, jumped up from his couch and begged them to share food and drink with him. He asked them to sit and they chatted for a bit while the server went for refreshments.

With his familiar wide smile, Snake said, "Soon you will be in school, Jaguar!"

"Yes, Lord," the boy answered respectfully.

"Will you go to telpochcalli to receive military training as your father did before you?"

"I don't really know, Lord."

Flower said, "May I speak, Lord?"

"Of course, Flower. Please don't be formal. We are all friends and old comrades. Oh, Flower, do you remember when we were traveling through the Earth on the underground river? Do you remember when I picked up that odd lizard with no eyes and it startled me so that I dropped it? Jaguar thought it was so funny to see me shout out! He went running after the lizard and we feared he would fall in the deep water! Do you remember, Flower?"

Flower's laughter tinkled merrily in the air. "Oh, yes! We needed to laugh then. We were in such a strange place! We didn't know if we would ever see the sky again!"

Snake's story worked to relax the two before him. Jaguar laughed out loud, saying," Oh, Uncle! I remember that, too! You screeched very loud and your arm jerked and the lizard went flying! It was very funny!"

Jaguar's face had lost the serious look it had when he came in. He said eagerly, "Uncle, I remember the jaguar, too. She pulled me from the water. She talked to me in my mind. Then, later, another jaguar talked to me. She thought I was her cub, and she wanted me to follow her, but I didn't."

Shocked, Flower said, "You didn't tell me about the second jaguar, Son!"

He answered, "There were a lot of things I didn't tell you about, Nantli. I was afraid you would watch me more closely, and I wanted to be in the forest."

Flower turned to Snake and said, "This brings us to why we came to you, Brother. We need your advice. You are wise in the ways of the Great One."

Intrigued, Snake looked at Jaguar and said, "Please tell me what is troubling you, Son."

After Jaguar finished telling his story of the cougar, he said, "This is why I said I don't know which school I will attend. I know most boys follow in the path of their fathers. My father is an honored Soldier—but Uncle—this cougar is the first animal I have ever killed. I know I could never kill a person. I cannot be a soldier or a hunter like my father. He has taken me hunting, and I always told him I didn't see any animals or that I missed the target. I am ashamed for being a bad son. If I don't become a soldier like him, he will be embarrassed by me. The other boys already tease me because I haven't had my first kill."

Snake felt badly for Jaguar, knowing how painful this must be for him. But, he was thrilled with the knowledge that Star's prophecy was coming true. The boy was able to converse with the animals, and he even healed one that was dead! What a beautiful gift the One had given him!

He said to the boy, "It is true that you should not tell untruths to your mother or father, but it is not true that you do wrong by not wanting to become a soldier! When you were a small child, Morning Star saw that you would be a great Shaman one day. What you tell me shows that you already have the gifts. This is something to be thankful for, Jaguar. It is a true blessing from the One! Now, you must learn how to use them. If this is the path you wish to follow, you must attend the school for Priests, the calmecac! Perhaps I speak too quickly, but I am sure Morning Star will agree when she learns all that you are capable of."

3

Feather felt lighter than air as she left the calli where Star's new baby had been born. She skipped through the door, hoping to find Jaguar close by. She wanted to talk to him about the new baby boy. Jaguar had been her best friend from infancy. He had always watched over her while the adults were working and building the city. He told her all the stories of the great journey that had happened while she was in her mother's belly. He told her that her mother, The Great Queen, and her father, Queen's Consort and the Leader of the Military, had led them from the great Aztec city of Tenochtitlan to their present home.

He told her about the great dangers they faced daily, but how they had always been protected. They had set out into the unknown world through jungles, underground rivers, and over mountains. They had faced the challenges because they had no choice. The Seers of Old had foretold that they had a great destiny, and that they were meant to found a new nation. Jaguar had said to her, "Feather, you have eyes just like the Queen. It was the Queen's blue eyes that marked her as the future Enlightened Ruler. The blue eyes were a sign that she was descended from Quetzalcoatl, the Prophet of Old, whom many worship as a god."

"But, Brother," she said, "my eyes are blue like my mother's. Why are mine blue, too?"

Jaguar said, "Because you, too, have a destiny, Little Sister!"

She thought about that now. Jaguar never did tell Feather what her destiny was to be. She thought, I wonder what it can be. Jaguar knows. He knows everything!

Unable to find her idol, the three-year-old girl felt the rumble in her stomach and remembered that she hadn't eaten. She went to the palace kitchen to ask for a snack.

***

Queen Mockingbird was glad that she was hearing the last petition of the day. As the city grew, she found that small disputes or misunderstandings sometimes erupted. If they were dealt with quickly, they didn't become a hindrance to the smooth functioning of the city. While Morning Star and Snake dealt with matters of Spirit, she dealt with the details of daily life. Once a week, Mockingbird sat on her raised chair in the receiving room. While petitioners came forth with problems, she prayed that she would be able to use her wisdom and guidance to solve these matters. She dressed for the occasion in tribute to the seriousness of the office. A headdress of magnificent quetzal feathers topped her gleaming black hair. A shift of the purest white adorned her slender body, tied with a belt of blue and green embroidered symbols. The white against her copper skin seemed to glow. Bands of gold, turquoise and the purest jade circled her arms and neck.

"Honored Queen, my husband and I seek your counsel." The woman stood facing Mockingbird, her eyes downcast as she shuffled her feet nervously.

The Queen said, "Pray tell me what matter disturbs you. Perhaps we can come to a solution."

As Mockingbird spoke these words, she watched the couple closely to see if she could discern what was being left unsaid. She was exhausted, but she was always careful with the power she had over others. She didn't want to risk misinterpreting the situation and to end up causing greater distress than they were already experiencing.

The woman said, "It is a matter that may or may not be of importance, My Queen. But, my husband and I are worried."

Mockingbird said, "Centehua and Cipactli, you are my people. I am here to help, so fear not. We live by laws, but they are the Laws of the One, and are not too harsh to bear. They are only in place to make our lives easier. I can see that you are nervous—perhaps, due to the intimacy of your problem—but I respect your need. Please explain what the difficulty is. If it is something I have no knowledge of, I will confer with my advisors."

She waited quietly while carefully observing the couple. The man, a strong-backed farmer, and his wife, a sturdy sunburnt woman, were out of their element in this sumptuous large room. The only others present were two servers. They were not slaves—but men who freely chose to serve the Queen. They stood to either side of Mockingbird, awaiting any instructions she might give.

Finally, the man cleared his throat and looked up at his monarch. "My Queen, I beseech you to forgive my roughness. This is a sensitive matter and it is difficult for me to speak of it."

The farmer took a deep breath, and blurted out, "The son of Ollin is my wife's cousin!"

Stunned with the news and wanting to know more, Mockingbird rose from her chair and slowly walked toward the two petitioners. The servers moved forward rapidly; but, as they began to walk them with her, she waved them back and said, "I will speak privately."

The two men immediately left the room.

Mockingbird said softly, "I thought never to hear that name again."

She looked down upon the man and wife who were several inches shorter than she was. The shock of hearing the name of Ollin after so many years gave her face a strange dazed appearance.

The woman answered her nervously, "My Queen, I would not have spoken the name in your presence...I never thought to...My Queen, please forgive..."

The man interrupted, "My Queen, my wife is stumbling over her words because she is ashamed to be related to the one with that name. But, Lady, we must warn you. My wife's cousin, Wolf, is a weak, spoiled man and would never do anything on his own."

The farmer paused, and then said, "But, my Queen, we have heard talk—dangerous talk. His wife—this cousin's wife—is a scheming woman. Always, she tries to be more than she is. She does this by causing trouble for others."

Mockingbird questioned, "My good people, how can this woman cause trouble?"

The farmer's wife said, "She can raise discontent, My Queen. She is spreading lies, saying that she and her husband are the true Enlightened Leaders of the city!"

Mockingbird replied, "And is anyone listening to her?

The woman answered, "Yes, my Queen. There are always those who like to cause trouble. Some are jealous, saying that you and the Seer, Morning Star, are but interlopers—foreigners who are trying to steal from us what rightly belongs to those of our village."

The farmer said, "My Queen, you know Ollin was named for a god. Some say he was born to lead the people and that you caused his death. They say that you were afraid of him because he was the destined leader. We know this isn't true, My Queen, but some will use this to try to defeat you."

Mockingbird remembered the Old Shaman, Ollin, from the fishing village. He had tried to kill her as they first entered the New City of the Door. Instead, his arrow had found the heart of the old priestess. Remembering, Mockingbird once again felt a pain in her own heart. Star had told her that Ollin knew of the power of the land and that he wanted to use it to rise to the Heavens. After his attempt to kill Mockingbird, he fled from her soldiers and was eaten by crocodiles in the river. Now, he appeared to rise from the dead in the form of his son, Wolf, whose wife wanted to usurp the power of the two Enlightened Leaders. *I must confer with the men,* she thought.

"One more thing, my Queen—if I might speak— my Queen, this woman, Mesquite—it is said that she follows the god of death!"

4

Eagle and Deer stood atop the high mountain to watch the sky. They had been on a peace mission for the Queen into the outlying areas. There were many small villages hidden in the rain forests. Many of the people of the outlying villages were unaware of the New City of the Door, and Mockingbird wanted to extend an invitation to them. A huge gathering and celebration would be held in the City to celebrate the new way of life and to thank the ONE.

Deer said, "It has been a long difficult time, but at last we are ready!"

"Yes," Eagle replied. "The People have worked diligently, eager to establish the way of the Enlightened Ones. Brother, do you remember how the City was almost hidden when we first arrived? The jungle held it in its arms. Vines and vegetation covered all of the temples, the palace, and the houses. But when we did finally enter it, we were welcomed loudly by the birds and animals, and the jungle released its hold."

Deer looked toward the City from the height of the mountaintop. "I wonder if Star's baby has been born yet."

Eagle smiled. "We will know soon. We should be home by tomorrow. It will be good. We have been gone long."

Deer said, "I imagine my son has grown since we have been gone."

Eagle replied, "Yes, Jaguar is growing rapidly. And my daughter is having a harder time trying to keep up with him."

The men smiled as they thought of their children. Jaguar and Feather were five years apart in age. Still, the close bond they had forged from the moment of Feather's birth was strong.

At the high altitude of the mountaintop, Eagle and Deer felt the cool air on their chests and arms as they set up camp for the night. They looked down at the top of the trees in the forest, and they were able to see for a great distance in every direction. After the fire was built and two birds roasted on a spit over the coals, they sat and watched the sun set over the village they had left that morning. It was the last of a long line of communities they had visited. They had been welcomed by most, but not all. Some feared them at first, but still extended hospitality while warily watching the newcomers to see if they could be trusted.

The men were weary, but with a good tiredness. After months on the journey of peace to the surrounding cities and villages, they were eager to be home. Both men knew they had accomplished much in the way of understanding with many new people. The welcoming ceremony would be large and it would last for several days.

While stopping for rest, they talked about the ceremonies they had held several years before, while on the long journey from the Aztec capitol to the New City. They had been a small and intimate group—but with a great power of unity and spirit among the tightly bonded travelers. There were several such ceremonies—naming ceremonies and the joining ceremony of Mockingbird and Eagle. There were sad ceremonies, too—the crossing ceremonies when the high priestess, Tlacotl, and the nurse, Singer, had died.

Every one had taken a great risk, but they all felt the risk was worth it. Mockingbird and Star would have been long dead by now if they hadn't had the courage to leave. Instead, they found freedom and their inner powers on the trail—powers and a destiny that would have never reached fruition if they had stayed where they were. Flower, Deer's wife, had picked up her child and what little she could carry from her comfortable household because she, too, knew that life wasn't safe where they lived. Deer and Eagle had deserted their military posts—where each had been leaders, respected and assured of high rewards. Snake had come with them, his reason being his great love for the teachings of Quetzalcoatl and his greater desire that all should be free to follow them.

The Welcoming Celebration that would be held for the new friends would be enormous. Hunters would go out to make sure there was plenty of meat of every kind, farmers would bring produce to the plaza, and others would build mighty cooking fires in pits. The musicians—singers, flute and drum players, and dancers would perform. Games would be played—ball games in the arenas, and foot races. What really excited them was the new ceremony of the naghol. It had been introduced to them on their journey, and the people of the land said they would bring it with them to the Celebration. The time was right, for the naghol was to be performed in the spring of the year. It involved building a very high tower around a tree trunk. The participants climbed the tower with very long strands of liana vines tied to their ankles. When they reached the top of the tower, they tied the vines to the platform and dove off, seeming to fly through the air, around and around like birds. It was a test of bravery, and an initiation for the youth of the country.

Many people from the surrounding villages agreed to come. They said they would bring special foods and drink with them. Yes, Eagle thought. It will be a wonderful ceremony! My wife will be well pleased. It has long been the dream of Mockingbird and Morning Star to unite many people under the Law of the One!

The men walked at a steady pace, eager to get back to the city.

5

Net's lean brown body streaked through the water, at one with the creatures who surrounded him. The dolphins were in a joyful mood, diving and jumping around Net. He grabbed hold of the dorsal fin of the largest female, Oona, as she came up for a gulp of air. Immediately, Oona dove deeply into the sea, skimming above the coral reef before rising to the surface again. Net opened his eyes to the wonder of the sea, watching the multi-colored schools of small fish, crabs, and other sea creatures. As Oona rose again for air, Net thrilled to the ride, watching the slowly gyrating sea plants and the jellyfish that hung in the water with their slender tendrils extended.

Net gasped and laughed joyously as his head broke through the water surface and into the air. Sunlight danced on the water, dolphins whistled, and water birds called. The sun was hot on his back, and he felt free.

Letting go of the dolphin, Net glanced toward shore and saw his father motioning for him to come in. Oona jumped into the air showing her pink underbelly and gave a squeal. A baby followed, and then the whole pod leaped into the air, one at a time. Net imitated their call, waved, and turned toward shore with long sure stokes of his gleaming arms.

Turtle, watching his son and the dolphins from shore, felt bad about calling Net in. The young man loved nothing better than the sea, and he had been forced to spend months at a time away from it while his father was recuperating from an illness. Turtle knew he probably would have died from his debilitating weakness if it hadn't been for the seaweed soup that his son patiently spooned into his mouth.

There had to be some healing property in the seaweed that Net instinctively understood. It was the only food that Turtle could keep down for several weeks; and then Net gradually added other sea life to the soup, until finally, Turtle's appetite and strength returned.

Turtle, born into a fishing village, was a trader by occupation. He traveled the length and breadth of the land, carrying seashells, textiles and art pieces made by the villagers. He traded these items for others found in inland villages. He was a good, honest trader and was liked by all he met—until the day when some soldiers wrongfully enslaved him. The gods had been watching his path. He knew this because Deer happened to meet up with them and he ordered Turtle's release.

Now, he thought about the strange sequence of events that once more brought him to the same camp as Deer. It was after Net's seaweed soup had brought him back from the edge of death. Turtle was concerned about not keeping up his trade route, so Net volunteered to go along with him. Turtle knew his son offered to go along so that he could make sure that Turtle was all right. He wanted to be there if his father needed him, even though his heart was torn between his father and the sea.

Turtle thought now of the day they had come across the camp on their way back home. Drawn by the smell of cooking meat, they hid in the forest and watched to see if these people seemed friendly. Suddenly, Turtle spied one of the men and was amazed to realize that it was the soldier who had released him several years previously. He was excited to see the good soldier, and planned to approach him to offer his gratitude and to learn if there was some way he could repay him. He and his son entered the camp unseen, and were suddenly startled by a woman who came out of the shelter. They ran off into the forest and hid again.

That night the campers held a Ceremony, and both Turtle and Net were awestruck to see the woman more clearly. She was dressed in royal garb and played a clay flute that sounded like music from the Spirit. They were able to see her deep blue eyes, so startling under her blue-black hair. Immediately, they recognized that she was the Enlightened Leader who had been long foretold by the Seers of Old.

Showing themselves, they offered their allegiance. They learned from the soldier that the blue-eyed leader was called Mockingbird, and that her sister, the Seer named Star, was also with them. Turtle and Net offered to lead them to their fishing village—and from there, on to the City of the First Men—the New City that was now named The City of the Door. It was the city that the prophecies said would be the new home to the Enlightened Leaders and their followers.

Watching Net as he walked from the sea, droplets of water sparkling on his skin and dripping from his hair, Turtle's heart swelled with love and pride for this young man who was his son. He remembered how, after they returned to their village with the Enlightened Leaders and their followers, the first thing Net did was to run to the water.

Turtle said, "Son, I have just come from The City of the Door. Trouble brews there. Ollin's son, Wolf, and his wife, Mesquite, are spreading discontent. I hate to draw you from your pleasure, but I must go to the aid of our friends. Will you go with me?"

Net answered without hesitation, "Of course, my father. Will we leave right now?"

"In the morning, my son."

6

Morning Star prepared herself before the obsidian mirror. Her servants had left after helping her to bathe and dress her hair. Now, she saw her reflection, resplendent in the shimmering turquoise, blue and green of her new shift. The light coming through the window caught the threads and changed the hue with her slightest movement. She had never seen such magical cloth before. It had been a gift from the trader, Turtle. He had told her that he had traded for it with strangers who said they came from across the sea to the east. The traders were very happy to receive jade carvings in return. The strangers had told him that the threads were spun by worms. Morning Star was filled with joy to think of all the ways in which the Mother created her gifts.

She moved before the mirror, captured by the dance of the rainbow that shimmered across her shift. A magnificent jade necklace encircled her neck, its large center pendant swaying between her breasts, and golden anklets tinkled as her feet moved. The action brought back the memory of her time as a dancer in the Aztec temple. She loved the dance—became lost in time when she danced—as she moved between the two worlds.

A faint cry from beyond the door brought her back to the present and she smiled as she recognized her infant son's plea for attention. The time had flown so swiftly! As she turned toward the sound, she called out for the nurse to bring in the infant. Taking him from his nurse's arms, she talked to him softly. As soon as he was in Star's arms and heard her voice, his fussing ceased. He had eaten right before she bathed, so after holding him for a while, she handed him back to the nurse to be put down for a nap.

His father, Snake, had given him the name of Tonauac (the one that possesses light). Shortly after Light was born, Snake held the boy in his two hands and looked him over thoroughly. He saw that the baby was watching him, his perfect little right eyebrow cocked up as though to ask a question. As Snake handed the baby back to Star, he had an instantaneous recall of another lifetime—and then he knew that this was a great soul in a small body. Pictures began to take form in his mind, coming toward him and receding, swirling in abstract beauty and then solidifying. He saw someone seated cross-legged on a floor of stone squares, perhaps marble. The man wore a tunic of white that seemed of one piece, and draped down over his knees. A belt held the fold of cloth in at the waist. He looked down and could see the pale feet, the light blond hair on the legs, and the edge of the white tunic. The walls in the room reached high to the arched ceiling, draped with many beautiful cloths. He didn't recognize the place, but he knew the man he watched had been himself at another time. He watched this man as he struggled with some kind of small instrument. He could see the hands working with it, and he wished he could recall what it was.

Then, through a large, arched doorway, another man entered the room. He had short curly hair, grey in color, a long blue robe, and leather sandals. A shawl of purple hue was slung over the man's shoulder, and tucked into the jewel-studded belt at his waist.

Snake could feel the young yellow-haired man's pleasure at the sight of the older man. He knew, somehow, that the older man was his teacher. He watched as the teacher walked toward him with an inquisitive quirk to his right brow. Squatting next to the younger man, the teacher was silent. His mouth didn't move, but Snake could hear his thoughts, "It is possible, Maran, that you are not considering every alternative. Start from the result, and work backwards. Then you can begin at the beginning and formulate a theorem."

Snake, in his present life, only had a vague understanding of what the teacher meant, but he could feel the sudden joy of the young light-haired man thrill through his body. He knew that his son was the honored teacher from that life, and the light-haired man's joy became his as his consciousness came back into the room. He knew that his new son was the same person he had revered in that distant lifetime. He didn't know where that had been, or when, but it felt as real as if it had happened a moment ago. He stood for a moment to remember all he could before he shared it with his wife, Star.

"It was the strangest thing," he said. "I could hear his voice, but he wasn't speaking with his mouth! It was as though his thoughts were mine—and I know I talked to him the same way! It was our son, my wife. It was Light who was my teacher!"

The Seer understood, and she wasn't frightened. She had visions of her own of past lives and accepted Snake's experience as natural. She had known intuitively that there was a connection—a bond—between her husband and new son, and now she knew from where it had come. Light would carry his mother's work forward—of this, she was certain.

7

Mockingbird stretched her arms high above her head as she removed the heavy feathered headdress. She had servants, but she liked her solitude when she had to think, so she hadn't called for them. Stripping herself of her sandals, shift and jewelry, she entered her bath. The warm water eased her tight muscles as the scent of flowers eased her active mind, allowing her to relax. She turned to her back and floated as she remembered her first bath in the Aztec temple after her parents had given her to the priesthood. Then, as a young girl, she had been at the mercy of everyone. Now, she was the leader of a large and thriving city.

She had power, but she was always alert to her inner intention, wary of becoming a slave to it. She knew how power could corrupt and destroy. Her old teacher, the Priestess Tlacotl, had told her, "Everything on Mother Earth can be used for good or evil. Hold steady to love and truth. Remember the teachings of the great Quetzalcoatl. Follow the Laws of the One God in Two Forms!"

The memories gently sifted through her stilled mind—pictures of Tlacotl and Snake telling about Quetzalcoatl's teachings. The One God had both a masculine and a feminine aspect. The masculine form was the active and creative force while the feminine form was the nurturing and inspirational force. The two energies made the One God complete, as the People would be when they would eventually come into balance.

Once she was completely freed of the stress of the day, Mockingbird walked from the bath and held out her arms while her servants oiled and dressed her in a simple and comfortable white shift. She slipped on the sandals that her dear friend, Flower, had made for her and waited for the servants to lace them up about her calves. Her dress completed, Mockingbird strolled casually from the bath area, and into a part of the temple she had only been in one time. She wanted to be alone, and decided a walk through this area would be entertaining. Perhaps she would find something of interest.

Mockingbird, carrying a lit torch, followed her instinct down an unused tunnel through several twists and turns. She had been here before, when they first arrived, but it had been a cursory inspection. Now, she walked slowly, searching for signs of any unseen doorways. She knew these tunnels had many secret paths, but some led nowhere. Searching carefully, she noticed a scraped area on the floor of the tunnel. She held her torch down to see if she could tell what made the mark. It looked as though something heavy had been dragged on the stone of the floor in a semi-circular direction. Then, holding her torch near the walls, she felt along the large blocks for any irregularities.

There! She thought, *This must be a doorway. Perhaps it leads outside through a secret exit!*

After much effort, she managed to find and pull a release that was hidden in a carved relief on the wall. A doorway appeared to magically slide open, following the marks on the floor. Mockingbird could feel her heart race in her chest at the new discovery. A fleeting feeling of someone watching her entered her mind. Immediately, she dismissed the thought, believing it was her imagination. When the door was fully open, exposing a side tunnel, Mockingbird stepped through, and walked for some distance. She memorized how many steps she took in each direction as she made her way through the tunnel. Then she came upon three doors—all closed—but she felt quite proud that she was becoming so expert at distinguishing the signs of new routes.

She decided it didn't matter which door she took, as she hoped to eventually investigate all of them. She noticed that two of the doors were quite visible, but the center door was almost hidden, even from her keen eye. This had to be the true door! She spent a long time feeling around for the hidden trigger to open it, and had almost given up, when she leaned against the wall to ponder the situation. She was drawn to a carved relief on the wall, and moved her hand to feel its texture. She must have triggered a secret mechanism without even realizing it—for suddenly, the door lifted straight up into the ceiling.

She peered into the entrance, but didn't see anything unusual. Taking a few steps inside, she decided she should go back before she lost her way, telling herself that she would come back another day. Mockingbird turned and retraced her steps through the tunnel, until she came to a dead stop. The door she had opened before was now closed. She had left them all open, and now she was sure that someone must have been in there, or followed her, and she was trapped. Over and over, she retraced her steps, until fatigue and desperation made her slide to the floor, still holding the torch, as she wondered how long the air would last.

8

As sunset drew near, Feather gave up on finding Jaguar and turned back toward the palace. She had searched everywhere. He wasn't at the homes of any of his friends, and he wasn't to be found anywhere in the market place.

Wherever Feather went, the people greeted her warmly. They were used to seeing her daily, as she loved to go around the city and see what was happening. This time, she was alone. Normally, a nurse, Jaguar, or the Queen, was with her. No one was overly concerned; however, that she was alone this day. This was her city and her people.

But now, it was getting late. Magnolia and Shell were on their way home when they spotted the child. Both had helped at her birth, and they felt an even closer bond and responsibility to her than most of the people. Picking up their baskets and moving quickly, they tried to keep the child in sight. Unlike her earlier leisurely stroll, Feather now moved rapidly, darting amid groups of people in the plaza, shooting around a crowd, and becoming lost to sight often. Flower was small, her three year old form easy to lose among the activity. Suddenly, Magnolia gasped. She grabbed her niece's arm.

"Shell!" The middle-aged Magnolia looked pale to her niece. She repeated in a voice of distress, "Shell!"

"What is it, Auntie? Are you ill?"

Looking about, trying to peer through the throng, Magnolia said, "Someone just grabbed Feather! I was watching her over there, and a man grabbed her arm. She seemed to struggle! Hurry, we must find her!"

The younger woman said frantically, "Where is she, Auntie? Who grabbed her?"

Still making way through the crowd, Magnolia answered frantically, "I don't know! I couldn't see who it was! We were too far away!"

As they neared the spot that she had pointed out, Magnolia said, "She was here! Here by this fountain! Oh, Shell, what can we do?"

Shell replied, "Auntie, calm down! Perhaps it was a server from the palace, just out to take the child home!"

"No, no!" Magnolia almost shouted. "It was someone I have never seen! His clothing looked like he was from a fishing village. He grabbed her arm roughly, and pulled her beside him! I don't see them anywhere!"

Magnolia was frantic. She had helped when Mockingbird birthed the child, and she felt as close to Feather as if she had been her granddaughter. Shell, too, felt a closeness and responsibility to the independent little girl.

She said, "Oh Auntie, we *must* find Feather! We *must!*"

They searched all around the fountain, behind gardens, and in a small partially open shrine. At last, they stopped in defeat.

Magnolia said, "We must tell the Queen what has happened. If the child hasn't returned home, they will send out searchers! Hurry, Shell! Hurry!"

Mockingbird still sat in the tunnel, thoughts all jumbled in her mind: *What happened? How could the door have closed? Someone must be behind this! Someone must have shut the door...No one will know where to look for me...I didn't tell anyone where I was going...Eagle...my husband...if I'm not alive when you return...Eagle, I will watch over you and Feather...NO! I will get out of here...I just have to think...reason...it is my talent...there has to be a way!*

Trying to clear her mind, she looked around from her seat on the floor. The damp chill crawled up her back and into her bones. *Why damp?* Her skin pulled tight, trying to hold in the heat, and little bumps appeared on her skin.

Forcing herself to rise, Mockingbird found a holder on the wall and inserted her torch into it. She rubbed her arms to warm them. The area she was in was small—a mere pass-through between larger rooms. Finally deciding she had to get up and move, she returned to the room she had just left—the one with the door that rose upward. It was a long tunnel, and she wasn't able to see to the end. Disappointment threatened to overtake her again, but she forced herself to keep going.

She could feel the slight decline of the floor—a slow gradual drop—as she walked slowly forward, trying to recall how many steps she had taken. After what seemed hours, she stopped abruptly. She had come to a dead end.

***

Eagle and Deer awoke just before sunrise. From the vantage point of the mountaintop, they could see in all directions. They saw the apex of the temple in the City of the Door, as it rose through the very top of the forest. After watching the sunrise over their city, they packed their belongings and set out for home.

Used to traveling through rough mountainous country, deep primeval forests, torrential downpours and the baking sun, the two men were in their element. They were hardened physically from the travel as well as the continuous training they set for themselves when at home.

"This is a good day," Deer said to his companion as they scrambled down the mountainside. They followed a well-traveled trail most of the way, but this trip to the top of the mountain was off the path. They had gone to the top to speak with Spirit. On the third day of fasting and prayer, both of them had received visions.

"A good day—yes!"

Eagle searched for a secure handhold as he came to a steep area, a sheer drop with no way apparent way around it.

It took the whole day for them to get back to the path, but the men were eager to get home, so they kept traveling. It would take them several days to get there. Much of the journey was done without talk. They were old friends, and knew each other so well that they had no need to fill the silence with chatter. Also, as soldiers, they knew how to keep silent, ever alert for sounds of animal or man. They knew the trail well, but it was difficult to see as they moved into the jungle. In the evening, the dense leaves blocked out any light from the moon, so they decided to wait until morning to proceed.

Two days later, as they neared the City, they both heard a sound that was out of place. Quickly and silently climbing up the nearest tree, they listened, alert for another sound or movement. It was a long wait, but their patience paid off as a party of travelers passed beneath them.

Eagle watched the travelers closely. He felt uneasy about this group, and wanted to know why. A heavy man led the way, his large belly protruding over his breechclout. His mouth hung open with exertion, and Eagle could see that his teeth were stained with the chicle gum he chewed. A front tooth was missing, and dried chicle stained the corners of his mouth.

Behind the fat man, a bony woman of indeterminate age walked, grumbling in an undertone. A medicine bag on a neck thong bounced against her chest, along with a necklace of bone. Her dirty hair was worn in the style of the people from the fishing villages.

Before he even formulated a thought about why they might be there, he was stunned with what he saw next. Behind the skinny woman, a younger man stumbled along, carrying a burden over his shoulder. He may have been the son of the pair, but Eagle didn't know or care—it was the burden that concerned him. Trussed up with cording made of a vine, his small daughter, Feather, lay over the younger man's shoulder. She appeared to sleep—her limp body hung like a dead weight as the man plodded along the trail.

Eagle let out a scream of rage as he leaped from the tree. He landed by the younger man, who dropped Feather to the ground and ran into the jungle. The older pair ran in opposite directions. Deer leaped from his tree and chased after the younger man. He had almost caught up to him; but suddenly, rain burst from the sky in a deafening downpour. Deer could barely see his hand in front of his face, so heavy was the rain, and he lost track of the man. Arriving back where he had started from, he found Eagle desperately trying to shelter Feather from the storm while releasing her from her bonds.

9

The Seer and High Priestess, Morning Star, knew it was time to resume her duties. She felt she had luxuriated in new motherhood long enough. Something was nagging at her to get back to work. She fed her child and, after kissing him on the brow, she handed him over to the nurse for his sleep. Then she prepared herself.

Although she was a wife and mother as well as one of the leaders of a growing city, Star was still child enough to enjoy the pampering and regalia that came with her position. She loved, too, the rituals and rites of her office. Many of them were new—intuitive rituals that she knew would help her to access her powers. Her abilities were ever expanding, amazing even herself when she took the time to ponder them.

The first step was always cleansing her body and spirit through the steam and water baths. All of the people used this means to clean away negative energies, negative spirits that might be lingering in their presence; but with Star, it was more. The mineral waters calmed her earthly stress, and took her into the presence of the unseen. She could feel when this happened. She felt overwhelmed with joy and oneness—Oneness with All That Is. That is the way she put it when she discussed it with Snake. He was a kindred spirit, and could understand much more than her words could convey. The bond between them was pure and deep—surpassing this lifetime and drawing on Time since the Beginning.

This is what she valued the most about her husband. She didn't have to explain things to him. Sometimes they even shared a Spirit experience. The first

time it was spontaneous. They hadn't expected such a thing
to happen.

At the time, they were far apart physically. Snake
had gone to the fishing village to visit Turtle as a special
envoy of Peace. Star had stayed home to help Mockingbird
with the leadership of the new City of the Door. There were
many decisions to make, and they had to be made by both
of them.

Star was ready to relax after a long day of
discussion, debate and planning with her older sister. They
both decided to go to the baths and forget about their work
for the evening, and they invited their friend and adopted
sister, Flower, to join them. They planned a pleasant
evening of food and conversation afterwards. It had been a
long time since the three of them had been together just as
friends—in fact, it had not been since they had traveled the
long route from the Aztec City to their new City of the
Door. After months of living together as a closely bonded
family, they were thrust suddenly into all the planning and
work of building this new place. With each of them having
their separate work, they lost much of the daily closeness
they had so enjoyed. Each of them missed the spontaneous
fun, and the times on the trail when they were all just
women together, chatting about the daily happenings. This
time together now, though it had to be planned, was to be a
reunion and remembrance.

When all three were in the steam bath, Star had
sprinkled herbs in the water that would be poured on the
hot rocks. A tranquilizing aroma arose with the steam,
washing around their bodies, and filling their nostrils. The
heat, the humidity, and the aroma had a hypnotic effect on
the three women. Mockingbird began to sing, her husky
voice throbbing in the silence. Flower and Star joined in,
swaying to the beat of the song. Suddenly, Star found that
her essence had left her body, and had risen to the ceiling.
From there, she looked down for a moment at the women

sitting on the rock benches. She was surprised to see herself sitting there, immobile, as though she had dropped off to sleep. She thought of her husband, and immediately she found herself in some other place with him. It was a large crystal temple, filled with bright glowing lights. She knew the lights were the spirits of others like herself who were drawn to this place, to be filled with beauty and understanding. Other, brighter lights were approaching, and she cried with the glory of what she experienced. Time stood still as she exchanged greetings with the others.

Days later, she told Snake about the experience. He told her that he, too, remembered being there. It had happened to him in the fishing village, when he went with Turtle to a ceremony led by another Shaman. He recalled everything that Star had told him about. They talked long into the night about all they had experienced in that crystal temple.

Now, thinking only of the warmth and relaxation, Star prepared for the baths. The steam was first—aromatic herbs to take her to a higher place so she might commune with the Spirits. Then the pool—mineral waters warmed deep underground, contained in a large pool, to connect with the Mother Earth. She needed both in her work as Seer and Priestess—the joining of Heaven and Earth. If she didn't connect to the world she lived in as she soared off to converse with Spirit, she would weaken the link and her spirit might not come back into her body to finish her work on earth. Her body could die. She wasn't ready for that yet. She had a city to help develop and a son to raise to manhood.

As Star entered the steam bath structure, she had an uneasy feeling. Something nagged at her—something was wrong—but she didn't know what it was. It was like something tugged at her mind, but then skittered out of reach and sight.

Star was an expert at clearing her mind and letting everything go. As she breathed in the aromatic steam, she almost immediately found herself in a place of calm nothingness. Time ceased to exist. She went deeper and deeper into Spirit. Gradually, she began to see a soft green glow in the distance. Slowly, ever so slowly, it came closer. The movement was a smooth flow, gradual and constant. As it came near enough to see, Star saw that it was the Crystal Skull that the Old Priestess, Tlacotl, had given to her.

Star had used the skull on the journey to the New City. She had used it to light the way through the body of Mother Earth on the underground river, and she had used it to heal her husband when he was poisoned by the jumping snake. Those were times when she intentionally used the power of the skull. Now, without her intention, the Crystal Skull—or its spirit—somehow came to her of its own accord. Star, in her state of deep meditation, knew that the Skull was a living thing. Pictures flashed through her view of its conception in the minds of the Old Ones. They had discovered a perfect flawless crystal and formed it into a repository of knowledge with the Magic of Old. It was in Aztlan, the place where the Creator had formed the first people. They had all the knowledge of the Creator, and they knew how to give life to objects.

Pictures flashed before Star of the long history of the Crystal Skull, and all of its properties. She saw how it could be used to heal, to foretell the future, and to help the Enlightened Leaders in their quest.

The perfect Crystal Skull floated before Star, its hollow eyes filling with green light—then changing to different colors according to the knowledge it imparted to the Seer. The changing colors emanating from the whole object imparted information that Star understood.

As she came out of her vision, Star knew what she had to do. She quickly thanked Spirit for the help, rose and walked down the steps into the pool, and rinsed herself.

10

Net hoped to see Shell when he and his father reached the New City of the Door. She and her aunt, Magnolia, had gone to the City to be with Star as she gave birth. They had delivered the Queen's daughter on the journey, so the Seer trusted them. Star had sent a special request asking for them to be her guests when her time was near. It was a great honor to be asked to preside at the birth of the Seer's child.

Shell had been excited when she told Net about the invitation. The two young people were close, and had begun to think about marriage. Usually, a woman was much younger when she married, but Shell had been patient. Net had gone for a long journey with his father after he recovered from his long illness. Then, when they got back, Net couldn't think of anything but the sea—fishing, swimming, and learning all the secrets of the dolphins. Shell waited and waited, trying to get him to look at her long enough to see what was in her heart, but his mind was elsewhere. Then, finally, he one day happened to really see her, and he fell instantly in love. She was so delicate, so sweet, and so lovely. Net began to walk with her, they started to make plans, and then the messenger had come from the City. He knew she would come back to the village after the birth of Star's infant, but he didn't have the same patience that Shell had shown.

Net didn't share this hope with his father, Turtle, as they journeyed. They were both silent most of the time, each with his private thoughts. Turtle was thinking of how long it was taking to get to the City, too. But, his impatience was due to fear for the Queen and the Priestess.

He thought, *I really shouldn't have left the City but I wanted to have Net with me, and I had to finish up my trade route. I should have forgotten about the trade route and gone to the Leaders with my warning. I hope I didn't wait too long!*

Turtle's mind swam with urgent thoughts and feelings.

I owe my life to them and to their soldiers. I must warn them!

He fought his way through the vines that had already started to grow over the path since he passed this way only two days before. The jungle was second home, and he barely heard the birdcalls and monkey chatter with his mind on his mission.

***

Eagle held his daughter close to his chest, trying to shield her from the sudden outburst of the storm. He laid her down underneath a large cluster of trees where the water was deflected. Putting his ear down near her face, he listened for breath but he couldn't hear anything through the noise of the torrential rain. He felt a thready pulse in her neck. Breathing a huge sigh of relief, he gently loosened her bonds, cutting the vines and tossing them aside with disgust.

Poor little Feather! My daughter, don't die!

As Eagle thought these things, he heard Deer come up behind him. Deer, an agile and skilled man of the forest, intentionally made noise so that Eagle would know he was there.

He asked gently, "Is she alive, Brother?"

"Barely," Eagle answered with a catch in his throat. "I think they gave her something to make her sleep." Then he said vehemently, "Our children aren't safe even here, Deer! What is the point of all of this? We talk of love and brotherhood. We say we are a nation of peace, but what I feel in my heart right now is not love!"

Deer looked down at the tiny girl and noticed her eyelids were fluttering, and then they stopped. He went to gather his and Eagle's packs.

Taking a blanket from his pack, he said, "Here, I will put this on the ground for her to lie on."

He watched as Eagle gently moved her to the blanket and soothed her hair back from her forehead. Eagle checked her arms and legs to make sure they were not broken, and then he turned to look up at Deer.

He said with anger, "Did you recognize those people? I think I have seen them at Turtle's village. How could they have taken Feather? I thought she was safe with the people of the City!"

Deer answered, "She has been safe, Eagle…for three years she has been safe with the people. They love her. No, I didn't recognize them, Brother. They must be outsiders."

The rain had slowed to a steady pelt.

Deer said, "I don't think we can travel in this rain. Hopefully, it will let up by morning. I will build a shelter so Feather will be warm and dry." He looked with compassion on his friend, wishing he knew how to answer his questions.

Eagle agreed to the plan. He didn't want his daughter to become chilled in her weakened condition. *Perhaps the drug she was given will wear off by morning*, he thought.

* * *

"I need your help, Husband!"

Star looked over her shoulder as Snake entered the room. She was dressed in full ceremonial garb, including her beautiful headdress, made of long blue and green quetzal feathers. A feather cape covered her shoulders. Her simple white skirt swayed with her movements as she continued to unfold the cloth from the object before her.

Snake moved around to see what she was doing, and saw that she had the object on a pedestal before her. The jade and gold of her necklace, set against the tan of her oiled skin, glowed as a shaft of sunlight came through the opening in the wall to illuminate her movements. She chanted as she revealed the object, letting the cloth under it drop to form a contrasting bed of azure for the clear Crystal Skull that rested upon it.

Snake felt a tingling sensation in his back as he watched his wife in her office of Seer and High Priestess. He, too, wore the garb of his office as Shaman. He joined in the chant, the prayer to the One, asking to see only the highest of truth and the wisdom to understand. He was The Snake Who Had Swallowed All Knowledge!

11

The black slits of the female jaguar's slanted green eyes held him transfixed while pictures flitted through his mind. *Come.*

The huge cat held his gaze, its body supple and strong as it stood on the low branch of the scrub tree. *Follow me.*

Did he hear her? Or was he imagining it? With one last long commanding look, the jaguar quickly leaped down and followed the trail deep into the forest. The eight-year-old boy couldn't help himself. He followed, running as swiftly as the trail allowed, stopping for only brief moments to check for her signs. Pictures of Feather entered his mind. He had to go. He knew he had promised his mother that he would stay within the city, but Feather was in danger. The female cat knew this, and she had come to lead the boy.

Jaguar's small body slipped easily through the trees, and deep into the forest, where towering trees cast a perpetual shade. He listened as he ran, not with his ears, but with his inner hearing. The spider monkeys were silly, not sensing the danger that Feather was in. The parrots were raucous and self-absorbed. He listened intently.

First he heard the feeling-thoughts in his mind: *Wait! I hear...she is there! Ahead!*

He immediately realized: Mother Jaguar is still talking to me...telling me to come...come!

Jaguar ran and ran, smoothly, silently, and quickly, as he had been running all of his life. He had the best endurance of any boy in the city.

A gigantic boa constrictor slithered across the path in front of him. He heard it talk as it moved away. *Don't step on me!*

The rain began slowly, not hitting directly on the boy as he slipped through the forest. The large leaves of the high trees protected him as the rain fell; but the path became slippery as the dead foliage on the forest floor absorbed more water. The birds and monkeys ceased their raucous chatter, leaving only the Mother Jaguar's voice in his head: *Come, my cub. Follow me!*"

***

Deep in the subterranean tunnels running under the palace, Mockingbird searched for a way out. Her throat and mouth were dry, her body chilled through. She ran her finger along the wall, where moisture seemed to seep out, and tasted it. It tasted clean, but there wasn't enough to test a larger amount. It did help though, to moisten her tongue and take the edge off of her intense thirst.

She could see no hint of another doorway, and she began to wonder if it was possible that she would actually be stuck in the tunnel forever—until her air ran out or she died of thirst and starvation. But, she refused to allow herself the thought for long.

She knew she needed to keep moving so the cold wouldn't seep into her body. She felt all along the walls for any kind of indentation or trigger. There were no carvings on the walls in this area of the tunnel. It was as smooth as the small obsidian knife that Eagle had given her so long ago, and which she now had strapped to her leg under her shift. It was in a flat leather sheath and readily accessible. She had grown accustomed to the feel of it on the long journey several years before. At the time, it had given her a sense of comfort when she was fleeing from the priests who planned to sacrifice her and Star to the gods. Now, it was a reminder of her husband's concern for her. She prized it more than anything except for the clay flute she had also carried with her on the long journey from the Aztec city to the City of the Door.

Deep in her memories, she almost forgot that she was looking for a doorway when, suddenly, she felt something.

***

Eagle felt the heat emanating from the body of his little daughter. She was feverish. She babbled incoherently as her eyelids fluttered, revealing the startling blue of her eyes.

He didn't understand it. Feather was never sick. *Maybe the drug they used was a poison*, he thought.

***

The rain still came down in torrents. It was morning, and Eagle's hope for a warm sunny day was dashed. He and Deer had constructed a small calli to shelter his daughter. Large leaves placed over the bent sticks repelled the water, and gave them a fairly dry place to lie. All night long, her spirit seemed to move in and out of her body. Sometimes she mumbled words he couldn't understand, and sometimes she seemed to be in a deep sleep. It wasn't a normal sleep, though. She couldn't wake up.

12

The terrible avalanche of rain slowed Jaguar as he broke through the edge of the forest and into the open area. It pelted against him so hard that his skin hurt. The sheets of rain blinded him, but he went on, with his eyes closed, listening to the voice of the Mother Jaguar in his head. He stumbled and fell, pulled himself upright, and went on. He no longer ran, but forced himself to push against the wall of rain, one painful step after another. He kept his eyes on the next tree, the next opening through the maze, the next hill.

He felt an urgency that he didn't take the time to analyze. All he knew was that his little sister was in danger, and he had to help her.

***

Magnolia and Shell hurriedly made their way to the palace, eager to warn Mockingbird of what they had seen. When they reached their destination, a guard took them inside. He left them with a servant, telling the man that they wished to have an audience with the Queen. The servant, an older man from their village, told them that the Queen was resting. He tried very hard to look dignified and proper; but the knobby bones in his old knee hurt badly. He knew that the rains were coming soon.

"Honored Father," Magnolia said. "It is very important that we speak to the Queen of what we have witnessed!"

The old man knew Magnolia. He knew she was a sensible woman and wouldn't get stirred up without a reason. He also knew the Queen had said she didn't want to be disturbed this evening. He wasn't sure what to do, so he told Magnolia that the Queen felt need of a rest, and asked if she could tell him what she had seen.

"Yes, Honored Father," she answered. "It is necessary that we see her immediately! Feather was in the market place and, even as we watched her from a distance, a strange man grabbed her by the arm and they disappeared into the crowd! We searched for her, but could not find her. We came here to see if, somehow, the little one came home. It frightened me, Father, and I had to know if the child is safe!"

Looking very concerned, the old man said, "Wait here! I will see the Queen and learn if her daughter has come home!"

He limped rapidly away, ignoring the pain in his right knee.

Magnolia and Shell paced the floor, waiting for the man to return.

***

Guilt and fear caused a sickness to well up in Turtle's body. He continued to push himself toward the New City with an urgency that couldn't be denied.

Behind Turtle, on the trail, Net began to worry about his father. He didn't look good. He had slowed down perceptibly; and when they stopped to eat, Net saw that Turtle's skin looked pasty. Turtle made an attempt to eat the dried meat and fresh berries that Net had picked, but he had no appetite. He sucked at the dried meat, hoping to gain some strength from it.

Net said cautiously, "Are you not well, my Father? You look a little pale. Perhaps we should spend the night here? It is a good place. You will feel better by morning."

They were in a large open area with scrub trees dotting the landscape here and there. The mountains could be seen in one direction, and the forest surrounded the open area.

"It isn't that far, Son. We had better go on. It's important that we tell the Leaders what is happening."

Turtle picked up his pack and set out again. All of a sudden, the hot sun disappeared behind the clouds. Net looked up and saw dark heavy rain clouds filling the sky. Thunder filled the air and lightning cracked loudly nearby.

Net said urgently, "It is going to be a downpour, Father. We better get across the river before it begins!"

Turtle felt as if he didn't have the energy to hurry, but he made the effort, and soon they were into the trees, and crossing the roaring water on the small swaying bridge. They knew that a heavy rain could wash the bridge out, as the river could overflow its banks and move with tremendous speed and power. The rain started when they were in the middle of the long bridge. The rain pelted their bodies, almost blinding them, and sending a chill to their bones. They hurried as much as possible, while trying to keep their footing on the slippery wood.

***

When the old servant learned that Mockingbird was not to be found and no one had seen Feather, he panicked. He hobbled up to Magnolia and told her that both the child and the Queen had disappeared. His knee was swollen to twice its normal size, and he winced from the pain.

Magnolia said, "Honored Father, please calm yourself. Perhaps you could sit down and rest your knee. You should not be on it when it is inflamed!"

"No, no, no!" he shouted. "I must find them! This is not right! Maybe the Queen was abducted, too!"

Magnolia said calmly, "Surely, not! I will go to find the Seer and her consort. Surely they will know where the Queen is! You sit there on the bench, Old Father, and do not rise or you may not be walking at all tomorrow!"

Unhappily, he obeyed Magnolia. She is surely right, he thought. He said out loud, "Perhaps the Queen is visiting her sister in her quarters—or perhaps they are both in the temple!"

Feeling much relieved at this idea, he put his sore leg up on a footstool that Shell provided for him. The skin around his eyes crinkled as he looked down with a soft smile at the sweet young woman who removed the sandal from his foot.

13

The rain beat against Turtle's weakened body as his foot finally found solid ground on the other side of the swaying bridge. Exhausted, he collapsed, sitting in the mud, and waited for Net, who had made sure his father crossed before he started out himself. The heavy storm loosened the anchors on either end of the bridge and Net feared it might not hold the weight of both men.

Finally, he saw his father step off the bridge and fall to the ground. Turtle faced his son across the rapidly moving river, shielding his eyes from the downpour. Hurriedly, Net set off across the wide expanse. Before he reached the other side, he saw three people approaching from behind his father. They hadn't yet seen Turtle where he sheltered underneath a tree.

Horrified, Net recognized the son, daughter-in-law, and grandson of the deceased Shaman, Ollin—the man who had tried to kill the Queen, Mockingbird, and replace her as the Leader of the City of the Door. For a moment, Net felt panic rise in his stomach. Immediately, he pushed it aside, and decided to act as if it was natural to be meeting the trio on their way back to the fishing village.

Ollin's son, Wolf, caught sight of Net coming across the bridge. He shouted, "Niltze! Hello! What are you doing out in this storm?"

The man's large belly jiggled as he laughed at his own remark. Wolf's bony wife, Mesquite, wasn't amused. She glared at Net and then at her husband. Their son, Zolin, looked more like his mother than his father. Tall and bony, with close-set eyes and thin lips, they both had an air of superiority—and of devious cunning. Wolf's name didn't fit him—he didn't seem to have the intelligence of the animal whose name he bore.

Turtle looked around to see who was calling out, and saw the very people that he had planned to inform the Queen about. For a split second, he wondered if it was too late. Then, he forced himself to stand and speak to them.

"Hello Wolf...Mesquite...Zolin. You had best stay under the protection of the forest. The rain is fierce."

"Ah, Trader! I didn't see you there," answered Mesquite. "If you know what is good for you, you, too, will seek shelter. I hear the rain god likes to take sacrifices in this river!"

Turtle didn't miss the underlying threat in the reference to her father-in-law's death three years before.

"We are leaving the river behind," he answered. Then he said, "We are on our way to escort the women, Magnolia and Shell, back to the village. They went to the City for the birthing of the Seer's child."

Net was impressed with the quick thinking of his father. They hadn't discussed ahead of time what they would say to explain their presence should anyone ask.

He said, "It seems the rain is slowing now. Perhaps it will be safe to use the bridge, now. We must be on our way."

They started on the path again, not looking back to see if Wolf's family made it safely or not. Turtle and Net did wonder, though, what the three villagers were doing there and what they were up to.

***

Mockingbird pulled the knife from its sheath on her thigh. She inserted the tip of it into the tiny indentation she had found in the wall of the tunnel. Nothing happened. Frustrated, Mockingbird went farther down the wall, feeling for anything different. The torch threw off a dim light, and it was difficult to see.

Mockingbird ran her hands along the smooth walls—as smooth as if a river had washed through the tunnel for years. She knew that underground rivers were abundant, and perhaps this tunnel had once been filled with water. Perhaps the river had been diverted long ago to make this passageway; or perhaps it had dried up. The thought of water made her throat ache for a drink. It had been hours since she had started off on her little excursion after her bath. She didn't know how long—she only knew that she was very thirsty.

She went back to the place where the tunnel wall had been damp. Again, she tried to capture some water for her dry mouth. It wasn't enough. She decided to use her knife to dig into the wall, hoping a little more water would seep through. She was getting light headed, and knew she needed to drink.

Careful not to damage the knife, she worked slowly, hoping to find a softer layer of rock; and finally, she began to make a small dent in the wall. After working for some time, she felt faint. She leaned her head against the wall, feeling the cold dampness against her face. Faintly, she could hear a sound in the ear that was against the wall. It was water! Moving water! Without thinking of the danger, she started digging again, hoping for a small trickle to come through from the other side.

***

Finally, the rain turned into a drizzle and the sun broke through the clouds. Jaguar stopped and listened. Hummingbirds! He followed their sound. It was different from the voice of the female jaguar he had been hearing. Tiny little voices—barely perceptible—not really words—pictures—fast moving pictures. He could see where they were.

The sun's rays shone through the leaves to brilliantly focus on an open area ahead. A sea of flowers gently bent and bowed to the hummingbirds and insects that fed on their nectar. Jaguar's body was so exhausted that he wanted to drop to the ground, but he knew he had to find Flower. He tried to concentrate on putting one foot ahead of the other. As he painfully moved through the tall sunlight flowers, he finally saw what he had been looking for.

Outside the calli, Deer was taking meat off the fire. It smelled so good! Jaguar's stomach churned in anticipation. With a new found burst of short-lived energy, he half ran, half stumbled, into the camp, fell into his father's arms and passed out.

When Jaguar came to, he found himself inside the calli, lying beside Feather. He could hear his father softly talking to Eagle outside. He felt refreshed, but very thirsty. He sat up and found a flask of water.

"The boy will probably sleep for hours," he heard Eagle say.

Deer answered, "He was guided here by the Great One…all those miles, through the rain! He could never have found us if he hadn't been guided!"

I will have to tell Father that Mother Jaguar led me, Jaguar thought.

Then, he looked down at Feather. His poor little friend looked so fragile, lying there. He felt a sudden urge to touch her, to see if she was still breathing. When he put his face close to her mouth, her breath tickled his cheek. He laid his ear on her chest, and could hear a raspy sound. He felt a flood of relief when he knew she still lived. Praying, he laid his hands on her, and asked to be given the power to heal her as he had healed the cougar. He told Spirit what a good little girl she was, and how much she was needed by her parents and friends.

Jaguar felt the power of Spirit move into the top of his head, down to his heart, and from his heart, down his arms—flowing through his hands, and into his young friend. Tears flowed down his cheeks, as he felt his brotherly love for her, and he pleaded with Spirit to heal her. At last, she stirred. Her blue eyes fluttered open. She smiled at Jaguar, and then closed her eyes again. He could hear her soft breath, regular and no longer raspy.

He pulled her covering up and tucked it around her shoulders. After kissing her cheek, he went outside to see his father and Eagle. Maybe they still had some of that meat that had been cooking. He was very hungry!

14

Net watched as his father painfully made his way up the hill. He could tell that Turtle was having a hard time. The older man seemed to struggle with every step, and several times, he slid backwards, only to catch onto a scraggly branch or a rock—and with great exertion, he pulled himself forward again and again.

At last, they reached the top of the hill where the ground leveled off. Turtle stood, panting as he waited for his son. He didn't feel well. The sky seemed to spin around above him, and he felt a cold sweat break out all over his body. He swayed and crumpled to the ground, his face slack, and Net ran to him.

Dropping to his knees beside Turtle, Net pleaded, "Father! Father, wake up!"

***

A trickle of water began to come through the crack in the wall, and Mockingbird lapped at it with her tongue. It felt so good as it moistened her mouth and soothed her dry throat. The water flowed more quickly from the notch she had made. Suddenly, she heard a loud groan and a sharp crack. She jumped back as the water forced its way through in a trickle. She looked at her feet, the soles wet, as the water continued to come through at a slowly increasing rate. She wondered how long it would take before it filled the tunnel.

Mockingbird scooped water into her mouth until her thirst was quenched. Then she renewed her search for an escape route. After painstakingly reexamining her route, she came to a place she had been before—the walls in this section were covered with writing. In her temple training,

she had learned to read and write the pictographs. The story
on the wall was about the Great Quetzalcoatl coming to
earth in human form to teach the People. She followed the
story along the wall, coming at last to the end. It told of
how Quetzalcoatl had sacrificed his earthly desires on a
burning pyre:

> *When the ashes had ceased to burn,*
> *Quetzalcoatl's heart rose up.*
> *They say it was raised to heaven*
> *And entered there.*
> *Wise men say it became*
> *The Morning Star, appearing at dawn,*
> *And they add that it was not seen*
> *For four days after his death,*
> *Whilst he had sojourned in the Kingdom of Death.*
> *And in these four days, he gathered arrows,*
> *And eight days later, he appeared again*
> *As the Great Star.*
> *Since then he has sat enthroned.*[2]

Mockingbird, initiate to the Mysteries, knew this
story was symbolic. It was a story told to the uninitiated
about the great soul who came to earth in physical form
back at the dawn of humanity. He came to teach the People
the Laws of the One God. The story of his self-sacrifice
was the simple version of how he transformed his body
through enlightenment. Mockingbird knew that the fire in
the story was actually the fire of his inner knowledge and
wisdom.

Mockingbird's hand moved along the writing as she
read, and suddenly, she noticed a piece of metal lodged in
the wall, down by the floor. She nudged it with her foot,
and to her amazement, a small part of the wall swung away.
Her first instinct was to run from the water that would
surely overwhelm her, but the panic subsided when none

came forth from the small opening. She knelt down and tentatively held the torch into the darkness. She stuck her head in and almost dropped the torch. Ahead of her in the darkness, a great cavern sparkled with riches.

***

Magnolia burst through the doorway to find Morning Star and Snake before the altar that held the glowing Crystal Skull. Frightened, she halted what she was about to say. The Skull glowed eerily, making her think it was bewitched. Magnolia stood, her mouth open in disbelief as she saw that it was not only glowing—it was moving and pulsating as the light waxed and waned. Unable to move, she waited and watched.

Morning Star and Snake stood before the frightening object and sang. Morning Star swayed and her feet moved to the rhythm of the pulsating Skull. It was hypnotic to Magnolia; she wasn't aware that she, too, swayed and moved her feet slightly as a force enveloped her—seeming to pierce her heart with a compelling, not unpleasant, agony.

She didn't know how much time had passed as she stood there, caught up in the ceremony, eyes glazed as she lost herself in the rhythm. She forgot all about her niece, whom she had left to care for the old servant. She even forgot why she had come here. The long quetzal feathers that made up the headdress of the Seer melted into a blur of blue-green. She merely existed as a spark of energy in the vast swirling stream that enveloped her. Then, the music stopped. The Skull was still and lifeless on the altar. Morning Star and Snake turned to her.

***

Now they followed the directions of the Crystal Skull as they made their way into the secret entrance to the tunnels, following the path of Mockingbird. In the lead, Morning Star held the Crystal Skull before her. It cast a glow that lighted directly in front of them. Magnolia followed behind, awe-struck to see the way the Skull seemed to direct the Seer. It threw out a spear of light to the right or left when she needed to turn, but when the path led directly ahead, it seemed to glow evenly, lighting the way. Unable to take her eyes from the strange object, Magnolia could hear Snake behind her. As he walked, he sang prayers to the Great One, asking for light in the darkness. She thought it was a strange request, for they already had a light. The Shaman was carrying a torch and the Priestess was carrying that eerie glowing object that Magnolia found so frightening.

***

The fire cast strange and ghastly apparitions behind the woman at the altar. The shadow of her long bony frame appeared to come forth and then to recede into the trees as she performed her magic. The air smelt of burnt offering—a putrid smell of rotted meat. The bones of her necklace clanked together with a dead echo as she performed her rites. She waved a bony arm and a large burst of colored smoke arose from the fire, throwing a macabre light over her masked face. The chanting of her followers grew louder, clashing with the screeches of the monkeys in the trees.

She threw back her head and shouted a prayer to the god of death, the mighty and fearsome Yum Cimil, whose adornment she copied. Skin spotted with black, looking decayed as the bones rattled around her neck, the skeleton of her body seemed to bear no flesh.

"Terrible and Mighty Yum Cimil," she shouted in a hoarse voice. "Come forth to help your supplicants. We are ever faithful to your ways and require your intervention now!"

Again, her long skeletal arm moved over the fire as another enormous cloud of smoke burst into the air.

She wailed, "The interlopers are trying to steal my power as they have already stolen the great city that is rightfully mine!"

She looked into the dark cloud of smoke, hoping for a sign that the god of death had heard her. The smoke seemed to take on a malevolent form. She heard the drugged celebrants gasp in awe and fear. *They see it, too!* She thought, *Ah, my power is great!* Her eyes gleamed in satisfaction and her mouth twisted into a superior smile. The god had heard her, and he had come at her bidding!

The feeling of power thrilled the woman. She knew there was no stopping her now! She looked over at her husband, Wolf, with disgust. *Oh, if only he was as great as I! So disgusting with his fat body and lazy ways! His father, Ollin, was great—could have been great—if only he hadn't been so stupid thinking he could overpower these foreigners without preparation! Well, he got his answer when the crocodiles ate him! Stupid man! I loved him. If only he had realized my worth and not given me to his fat son when he tired of me. He didn't know what he was losing!*

She looked up with yearning at the form in the smoke. Her god—her god of death—from which her power came. It was an evil twisted thing that fit her distorted soul perfectly. She pulled a knife from its sheath and offered blood from her arm to the creature in the smoke.

15

Mockingbird squeezed through the low portal into the large cavern. For a moment, she wondered if she was hallucinating. She knew she had been in the tunnels for a few days. Perhaps the stale air and lack of food and water had given her a fever. Maybe she was losing her mind! No, it was real!

It was too much to take in all at once. She dropped against the wall, sliding to a sitting position. The torch was almost burned down. It wouldn't be long before she had no light. What a trick she had been played—to come to this vault of riches and die here like a poor lost soul.

She wondered if she had somehow gone against the teachings of the One, or if she had abused her power somehow. Why would she come to this end? She was weak and tired. She hadn't slept since entering the tunnel—only short restless naps for a few minutes at a time—only naps filled with troubling dreams.

Shrugging off the discouraging thoughts, she looked around. The cavern was very large, extending for at least a hundred yards. The ceiling of the cave was so high that she wondered if she was now inside a mountain. She gazed around at the splendors before her: statues of gold and caskets filled with jewels. Carvings in jade, turquoise and obsidian lined the walls. *This must be the storehouse of the legends*, she thought. She recalled the songs about the ancient ones who had built this city. When the soothsayers said that a mighty army would overrun them, the king had his army hide the wealth, and they snuck away before the invading army arrived. Now, Mockingbird knew the song was true, and this is the place where the ancient king had his men hide the treasure of the City.

As Mockingbird prepared herself for death, she felt no fear. She knew it wasn't the end—that life did not end. She wasn't afraid. She had left her clay flute in her quarters, so she sang. It was a song of gratitude for the beauty of the Earth, for family and loved ones, and for the One God who had given her the gift of life.

***

The water, pushing rapidly through the wall, was up to their knees; but the Priestess proceeded along the path, led by the glowing Crystal Skull. She could feel Mockingbird's calm presence nearby. Then she heard her voice. The Queen was singing to the One, thanking him for all the blessings of life, and anticipating the crossing into the other world.

She felt an urgency to get to Mockingbird before she decided to depart from her body. It was close, so close. Now she followed the beautiful voice, merely a whisper through the thick wall, but she could see no torchlight ahead.

Behind Morning Star, Magnolia whispered, "My Priestess, where *is* she?"

Just then, the Crystal Skull threw out a spear of light ahead. It pointed to a place under water. Morning Star hurriedly moved forward. She felt the wall with her foot, finding the opening under the water. The Skull continued to point the way, and Star knew that she would have to follow. Without a pause, Star firmly tucked the Skull under one arm, ducked down and swam through the opening in the wall.

Magnolia turned to Snake. She said, "I can't, Shaman! Even though I was born to a sea village, I am deathly afraid of water! I almost drowned as a child…" Her voice dwindled away, her shame too strong.

"Wait here, then, Lady," he answered, handing the torch to Magnolia. Immediately, he followed his wife, ducking down into the water, and finding his way through the wall. Magnolia stood alone, holding the torch against darkness, and she waited.

Emerging on the other side, Snake's first sight was of his wife holding the Queen in her arms. Relief flooded through him. When he looked about, he couldn't believe his eyes. The glow of the Crystal Skull illuminated most of the cavern. The light reflected from the gold and from the sparkling jewels—throwing rainbows of color on the surface of the rising water.

16

Deer carried Feather on his shoulders as he climbed the hill. On the other side, he knew, they would be able to see the City. Suddenly, he heard a voice calling to him from the distance. He stopped, putting his hand above his eyes to shield from the harsh sun. Coming up from behind, Eagle and Jaguar followed suit.

"It's Net," Deer shouted. "The son of Turtle!"

Net began to run toward him, shouting, "Soldier, my father needs help!"

The mother jaguar's voice was heard in the forest—an eerie and mournful sound—as Deer and Eagle ran forward to meet Net. Eight-year-old Jaguar, suddenly spurted forward, passed Net, and disappeared into the trees. By the time the adults caught up to him, Jaguar was kneeling beside the prostrate body of Turtle.

Eagle lifted his little daughter down from his shoulders and she ran to the boy's side. When Jaguar turned his head to look up at his father, Deer saw the tears that rolled down his son's cheeks.

He dropped down beside his boy and asked, "What is it Son?"

Barely able to speak through his pain, Jaguar said, "My father, the Trader woke up. He told me he had dreamed of people who prayed for the death of all who follow the One. He told me he had seen them in a forest glade, praying by a fire. Trader told me that his spirit was strong, but his body was weak. He said he felt his body slipping away, but that it was the way it was to be. He said that he will help us from the Spirit world."

The tears continued to stream from Jaguar's eyes. Never again would they see the stocky little man with the muscle-toned legs as he entered the city with his sweet toothy grin and shouted out the news from far places.

Net dropped to the ground, his grief almost too much to bear. He and his father had become so close when Net had healed him with the seaweed soup, and even closer on the long arduous trade route afterwards. He couldn't imagine life with the knowledge that he would never hear his father's voice again, or walk with him on the jungle trail, or to see him watch from shore as he swam with the dolphins.

Net felt Feather's small warm arm caress his shoulders. The innocent child's comfort was more than he could bear, and he dropped his head to his father's still chest and sobbed.

***

Mesquite looked around at her followers with disdain.

Drunken fools!

The fire had died down to ashes over the night. Bodies sprawled everywhere, as if they crumpled to the ground without plan. She pushed at her husband with her foot. When he didn't budge, she spat on the ground, barely missing his face.

She thought, *At least they have served their purpose.*

In the midst of her ceremony to the god of death, she had seen a vision of the trader's death.

Pitiful little man, she thought. *How he fawned over the usurpers! He won't bother me anymore!*

She felt a sudden chill. Looking at the sky, she saw a dark cloud skim over the surface of the morning sun.

Her son was awake. He pulled himself off the ground, and headed to the trees. When he finished, he sought out his mother.

MORNINGSTAR RISES
Doorway Series Book II

She said to him, "We aren't done. There is more work to do and more plans to make."

***

Shell didn't know what to do after she had helped the old servant to bed. She was alone in the room reserved for those who wished to speak with the Priestess. She fondly remembered the birth of Morning Star's son. It had been a great honor when she and Magnolia were asked to come to the City to preside at the birth. When the baby was born, she was the one who caught him as he came into the world. He opened his eyes immediately and seemed to stare at her as if he knew her. He was such an alert baby, seeming to be aware of all that was around him. This was most unusual for a newborn infant.

Her mind wandered to Net, the young man she had loved for years. She wondered if they would ever have a child together. The yearning was great in her, and she was getting on in age. She was two years older than the Priestess, and still had not been with a man. Many of her friends were already wives and mothers, and they had all freely coupled with various boys before making their decisions. She wondered why she had not done so. It was the way that all girls knew what they wanted, but she had known from early in life that she wanted Net, and only him.

Her earliest memory was standing in the shallow water with the other children. An older boy yelled at someone far out in the sea, telling him to come back. That was the first time she remembered feeling the fierce yearning for the boy in the deep water. He had grabbed onto the dorsal fin of a dolphin, and it had taken him far out past the safety of the shore. Out, out he went until she could only see a small dot. They all thought he was lost forever, except for Shell. She knew he would be back, and when she saw the dolphin bring him closer, she jumped up and down in the water and laughed. She had been very young, and he hadn't been much older.

Finally, the boy let go of the dolphin and began to swim to shore. At last he reached the shallows and began to wade in as the bigger boys chastised him severely for his bad judgment, and threatened to tell the elders. Shell's eyes had glowed proudly as she saw how little he was concerned with what the elders were told. She wanted to go with him out in the deep sea, holding his hand as the dolphin took them out to where the water changed color.

Shell rose up from the seat she had been in, and paced the floor. Her mind reverted to why they had come to the Palace. Once again, fear tugged at her. Little Feather was in danger. She had been abducted, and they didn't know where she was!

Who could have taken her? Why would anyone take her?

These questions wouldn't leave.

Now, she remembered being at Feather's birth with her Auntie. Magnolia had offered to assist at the birth, and Mockingbird had agreed with relief. The Enlightened Leader of today had been a nervous child who hadn't known what to expect, and Feather's Aunt had a way of calming women in childbirth.

Shell remembered, too, the first time she had seen Feather open her eyes. They were a startling blue in contrast to the tiny brown body with the shock of black hair. Just like her mother, everyone said. Yes, she remembered that birth clearly, even though she had attended at so many since then. She had even gone on her own to perform the duties when Magnolia had been sick or away from the village.

Something about that infant had struck at her heart with fierce protective love. She knew she would seldom see the baby again, but she would never forget her. Then, when she came to the City with Magnolia, she got to know the little girl. Feather came to visit soon after they arrived. She asked so many questions! Shell smiled to think of the child's curiosity.

Feather had visited Shell one day soon after they arrived. She had a regal air that was unconscious. "Tell me, Shell. Tell me again of my birth," the little girl had demanded with anticipation.

Feather sat comfortably at the table as Shell offered the little one some dried fruits and coconut milk. The girl nibbled and sipped daintily as she listened. Shell made quite a story of it, telling her about the weather, the small calli that had been constructed for the occasion, and who all was there at the time. She remembered to tell Feather how her mother and father had been so proud to have such a strong fine daughter.

It had been a wonderful day. Feather asked many questions about birthing, and Shell tried to answer her in a way she could understand. Feather also had many questions about life in a fishing village, and Shell suggested that perhaps she could visit them one day.

Feather left, quite satisfied with the visit, and promised to return another day.

These were the things Shell was thinking of when Net appeared. At first she thought she was dreaming. Then she saw how bedraggled and tired he looked.

She stood, unable to speak, and waited.

17

The group of friends who had come so far together met in a private room of the palace. They had made it back to safety and rested for a few hours. The children still slept, watched over by the nursemaids.

Plans were made for Turtle's funeral and stories were exchanged. As each shared their individual experiences, it became apparent to all how severe the danger was. Mesquite would stop at nothing. When the plans to abduct Feather and kill Mockingbird didn't work, she turned to magic, and she had caused Turtle's death.

Eagle wanted to track down Mesquite and her followers. As a soldier, he had been skilled in strategy and he had led others in battle. He had already begun to form a plan of attack. Deer agreed, and was ready to handpick a troop of soldiers whom he trusted. He would be Eagle's second in command and was ready to fight to the death for his people. Eagle requested permission of the Leaders to follow through with the plan. The Queen and the Priestess did not answer, saying merely that they would hear the rest of the stories before making a decision.

Net was eager to join the soldiers, even though he had no training in warfare. He only wanted to see them all pay for his father's death. Shell watched Net with fear as he spoke, afraid that he, too, would die.

The Shaman, Snake, was the only one of the men who didn't jump to the attack. He had such a firm conviction that life was about love, not war. He knew there had to be a way to stop Mesquite and her god of death without causing further loss of human life.

Each spoke in turn, giving his thoughts to the group.

The women, too, spoke. Magnolia told them what she knew of Mesquite and her followers. She had lived in the fishing village all her life, and had watched Mesquite over the years. They were the same age. She told how Mesquite had always been consumed by power.

Magnolia recalled that Mesquite had always been an awkward, unattractive girl, jealous of everyone, and a troublemaker.

Magnolia mused, "If she had been a sweet-tempered girl, she would have found friends and happiness; but she was cruel. She thrived on stirring up trouble."

Mockingbird asked, "What kind of trouble, Magnolia?"

"For one," Magnolia answered, "she stole things that belonged to others. Then she blamed someone else. Once, she took a beautiful pair of sandals from one of the girls and put them in my belongings. It must have been her, because she led others to my home and demanded a search."

"It was terrible," she went on. "But, luckily, no one believed I would do such a thing. The whole village was aware that there was something not right about her. She was cruel to smaller children. She teased them un-mercifully."

"When she was a young woman, no man wanted her; but she was cunning. She had her eye on the Shaman, also a crafty person. He had power, and people were afraid of him. She wanted to share his power. Her problem was that the Shaman was married, and she didn't want to share the power with the Shaman's wife. She wanted him to herself so she could bend him to her ways.

I don't know how she did it, but she managed to kill the Shaman's wife. Perhaps the Shaman, himself, aided her. You know his name—Ollin—meaning Movement. It is a powerful and good name, but he perverted it. It had become a name to be feared. He, too, craved power.

Somehow, Ollin's wife became ill and died. It was very sudden. Some asked each other in whispers, "How is it that such a powerful shaman couldn't save his own wife?" But they were afraid to ask him directly. They thought they knew the answer, and they didn't want to be the next to die."

Magnolia shifted in her seat, leaning forward with widened eyes, and whispered, "No sooner had the Shaman's poor wife died, than Mesquite was in her place. Ollin didn't marry her properly, but she took over as if he had. She started wearing her bone necklace, and acting as though she was the Shaman, and not he. Ollin tired of her eventually and gave her to his son, Wolf."

Net said, "I know their son, Zolin. He was always slow like Wolf; but like Mesquite, he is greedy and self-important. In our village, we are taught to care for those who can't care for themselves; but when any of the children tried to show Zolin how to do things properly, his mother would stand nearby and shout insults at them. After a time, it seemed that he believed he was better than the rest of us, so no one wanted to be friends with him."

Eagle said, "He must have been the one who was carrying Feather."

Mesquite answered, "Yes, from the description you gave, it was Zolin. You say he ran off?"

"All three of them ran away! Such cowardice! Stealing a child, poisoning her, and running away!"

Snake said, "One of them must have closed the doorway in the tunnel after the Queen entered. I could see no other way that the door could have closed. They have been very busy. They tried to kill the Queen, they kidnapped Feather, and they used evil magic to destroy our gentle friend, Turtle."

"They must be stopped!" Deer said. "I don't see any other way than to go after them with a unit of soldiers!"

Morning Star said quietly, "There is another way, Deer. Let us remember who we are and why we have come here to this beautiful City. We are followers of the Laws of the One God, as taught to us by Quetzalcoatl!" Her voice became firm and passionate.

"We are a People of Peace and Light. We cannot become that which we despise. We must live true to our beliefs!"

Eagle asked her, "Priestess, tell us how we can be true to the ways of the One and still stop the god of death from taking our people before their time. How can we protect you and the Queen and the children? Do we just sit back and watch as Mesquite employs her wicked arts?"

Star replied, "I understand your frustration, Soldier. I know it seems contradictory to you, who has been raised to fight for your beliefs. We can still fight, but we must be armed with the Sword of the Great One. It isn't a sword of obsidian, sharpened to kill at the swing of your arm."

"What is it then, Priestess? I beg you to enlighten me. Yes, I am frustrated! I was away on a peace mission when the wicked one came into our midst—into our peaceful city—and tried to kill my family. I feel as though I am useless to my family and to my city. Tell me, then, what purpose I have. What can I do?"

Star took Snake by the hand. She said to Eagle and Deer, "While you were gone and, before I heard that the Queen and her daughter were missing, I had a vision in the bath. It was a vision of the Crystal Skull. I asked my mate to accompany me to the temple to commune with the ancient Receptacle of Knowledge."

Snake took his cue from Star. He continued her story: "The Crystal Skull was created by the Ancient Ones, before the knowledge was lost. It is a tool to help us remember. It contains great stores of knowledge; but more than that, it is a living thing. It is capable of learning and teaching. It can be used in healing the sick and dying.

There seems to be no end to its uses and abilities. It is truly an amazing thing, but not a god to be worshipped. Even with all its many secret talents, it is still a tool. It was made by our ancestors, who were men and women like us."

He looked at each person in the room carefully.

Then he said, "The Crystal Skull can only be activated by Seers of great talent. In this generation, the only one who can make the Skull work is our Priestess, Morning Star. There is a connection between her and the Skull that causes it to awaken."

After a brief pause, Star said, "After I had the vision that told me that the answers to my discomfort were contained within the Crystal Skull, I knew what I had to do. I have been lax in my duties in my last months of pregnancy and for a time after the birth of our son. I knew it was time to lay down motherhood for a short time and take up the role of Priestess.

"I asked my mate to accompany me in a Ceremony to Awaken the Crystal Skull. He agreed gladly because we are as one in purpose. Both of us were transported to another place and time. We understood much that is happening today because we know what has happened in the past times. We were taken between lives, to see and hear what we understood fully then."

Everyone in the room had ceased to move as they listened intently. As adopted members of the royal family, they were privy to the daily events of the two Enlightened Leaders, but this was different. This was a gift of great magnitude—the sharing of Spiritual knowledge and experiences.

18

Morning Star looked into the eyes of each person—each one a trusted family member and friend dedicated to the Law of the One God in Two Forms. Then she spoke as she walked toward a covered pedestal:

"We have been given permission to share this knowledge with you. Each and every one in this room has raised their individual consciousness to a high level so you are capable of understanding! We are as one in our intention and belief!"

With that, she pulled the covering from the Crystal Skull. A soft humming sound emanated from it, and a rapid vibration was visible. Slowly, a light began to project from all around the Skull. First it was the familiar green, followed by other, higher, colors: blue, violet, gold. It was like watching a rainbow form, and all of them gasped in awe.

Shell watched Morning Star as she began a slow dance, accompanied by the soft throaty song of Mockingbird. The music, dance and lights all speeded up until a crescendo was reached—then it was suddenly and completely still. To Shell, it felt as if time, itself, was suspended. She waited, not breathing, not aware that she was waiting. She just *was*. A tendril of thought floated through her awareness: *This is what it is like for Net when he is riding with the dolphins.* The thought was gone, and then there was nothing.

Now she felt lifted from the floor, rapidly moving through space, and she could see lights all around her. She knew the lights were her friends, and that she looked the same to them. They gently settled into a huge crystal pyramid—a holy place—and she felt the love that surrounded her. She saw and heard the high teachers, brighter lights than even her friends, as they instantly imparted knowledge to her. She felt the bond with all that is, and she knew that she had never been alone.

Then the Crystal took them to a time ages back, when the Mother Earth was new. The skies were steamy and the water covered everything. Suddenly, she was soaring over the water, and she saw the water divide as land appeared. She looked around and saw the lights—the same lights she had seen in the crystal pyramid. All of her friends were here with her, at the beginning of time.

She found herself back in the pyramid. .No sooner did she realize it than she was once again over the earth. It was changed. There was much more land with huge animals roaming over it, and the sky was blue with wispy clouds scattered across it. She entered the clouds to experience the difference. Then she shot down to the earth and the light-that-she-was entered into an animal. She wanted to know what the animal experienced. Suddenly she was very hungry. She had never before known hunger. She felt a heaviness of body, heard a crunching as the animal moved, smelled the warm humid air, and tasted the vegetation in her mouth. All of these sensations were stimulating beyond anything she had ever experienced.

Shell didn't know how long she roamed the new earth within the large animal. Somehow, she was suddenly back in the pyramid. In an increasingly rapid cycle, she lived one experience after the other. Each trip took her to a different lifetime, her senses all telling her that the lives were real.

She washed clothes with other women in a river in a hot steamy land. She was one of a group of male hunters in a temperate climate, wearing shaggy clothing made of skins. She was a female child playing with other children on a tropical beach. She was a middle-aged man with white hair, wrapped in a white toga, speaking decisively before a group of like-appearing men. And in between lives on earth, she saw herself in various forms in alien-looking places that weren't earth-like at all; but even these experiences were as real to her as the one of her present life.

She understood completely the cycle of rebirth and saw what she had done right and wrong in each experience. At the same time, she saw how her whole group interacted among themselves and with others in each time and place. She understood how she became the woman, Shell.

Every person in the palace room experienced his or her own cycle, just as Shell did. Each one finally understood everything. It was a knowing beyond the ability to verbalize. It was a remembering.

Now, they all saw the past, present, future at the same time. There was no such thing as death, only a changing—a constant flow from one form to another. They created their own destinies. The group in the room was armed with the sword of The Great One, and had the power of the Law of the One God.

Even Mesquite and her followers were in their own cycles, and they were experiencing what they had created for themselves. Where the cycles overlapped—where the two groups interacted in the Now—this is where the destiny could change as they continued to create.

19

Mesquite hadn't been idle. Driven from some dark place within herself, she had a desperate need to always be right, to be the one in control. This need energized her and gave power to her desires.

The spark of the divine within Mesquite was almost drowned out by this desperation, born of her thwarted need for love and respect.

***

Alone now, Morning Star peered into the depths of the Crystal Skull. It was still now—opaque and lifeless. She cupped the skull with her hands, asking the One to use this Ancient Tool to show her how she could protect her loved ones from Mesquite. Slowly, a picture formed deep inside the skull. She could see Mesquite moving and gesturing to someone. Squinting her deep brown eyes, she watched Mesquite intently. For a moment, she saw a small light inside of the woman. It appeared for a second and disappeared, again and again, like the rhythmic light of a firefly.

Morning Star knew that Mesquite, too, held the Divine Spark. It was hard to see, so small and shrouded was the light with its overlaying of selfishness, but it was still there. She wondered if there was some way she could help Mesquite to recognize that spark within herself—some way she could help her to know that they were sisters and were there to help each other.

The Skull began to warm in her hands. The pictures became clearer. She watched as Mesquite birthed her son, Zolin. She could feel the contractions in her own body as she watched the woman struggle to give birth. The narrowness of her hips, her anger at her husband's dead father for impregnating her, and her fear of the unknown, all caused the birth to be much harder than it should have been.

As Mesquite struggled, she was in and out of consciousness. Morning Star followed Mesquite, struggling along with her. As Mesquite appeared to lose consciousness to the world, she was conscious in another time, reliving all the painful memories that had surfaced.

She felt Mesquite's horror when Ollin coldly turned her over to Wolf. Reaching into Mesquite, Morning Star knew that it wasn't only the power that Mesquite yearned for. Even Mesquite hadn't been fully aware that a yearning for acceptance and security inspired her desire for Ollin. No one had ever really loved her, and she mistook Ollin's sexual advances for love. Then, in the end, she knew that he didn't care.

Wolf, her slow and stupid husband was actually proud of her. He didn't realize that she was pregnant by his father—and she didn't realize that Wolf loved her. If she had known this, she could have been saved at that moment. She could have found some meaning in her wilted life.

Now, Morning Star followed Mesquite back even further, to her childhood. She felt the hardening in Mesquite as she finally realized that her parents despised her. She had known the humiliation and pain since her birth, wondering why she couldn't please them. She tried so hard, but nothing she did was right.

Mesquite's consciousness asserted itself briefly, and she screamed with a force that caused the hearers to shudder. Then, she slipped away again... back to before she was born as Mesquite.

Mesquite's mouth screamed and screamed again; but her soul was somewhere else. Morning Star was still with her, feeling the horror and agony over what Mesquite had done as if it was her own.

Morning Star realized that Mesquite was between earthly lives, suspended in a violent space. She experienced the slowly awakening understanding of her past life. It was one in which she was very powerful—very gifted—and blessed with everything she could desire. She had built this bounty with her thoughts and actions over many lifetimes.

The terrible agony Mesquite experienced was in the knowledge that she had let her blessings be her downfall. She had used her power unwisely and selfishly. She was determined to rectify her errors in the next earthly life. She would be born less than attractive physically, and she would be born to parents who weren't apt to spoil her. She would be born into a small village to parents she had wronged in past lives. This would give her the opportunity to overcome her belief that she was superior to others.

Morning Star once again was with Mesquite as she struggled to give birth. At last, her son was born. Morning Star forced herself to separate from Mesquite. She was still with her enough to feel the overwhelming love that Mesquite felt for her son, Zolin, but Morning Star was also aware of herself. She knew that, in that moment, Mesquite totally forgot the between-life memories. She only saw, heard, and felt this little baby boy—and he became the focus of her present life.

Morning Star saw now that the only way to reach Mesquite would be through the one person she really loved — her son Zolin.

PART TWO

What does your mind seek?
Where is your heart?
If you give your heart to each and every thing,
You lead it nowhere: you destroy your heart.
Can anything be found on earth?

Beyond is the place where one lives.
I would be lying to myself were I to say:
"Perhaps everything ends on this earth;
Here do our lives end."

No, O Lord of the Close Vicinity,
It is beyond, with those who dwell in Your house,
That I will sing songs to You, in the innermost of heaven.
My heart rises;
I fix my eyes upon You, Next to you
beside you, oh Giver of Life.[3]

1

Morning Star stood beside Mockingbird at the top of the extremely high stairway on the side of the temple. From this height, they could see the mountains and the sea. They stood where the temple pinnacle sat high above the tops of the jungle trees. They had come up here to pray for peace and abundance; but now, they watched the bustle of the city below.

The plaza was a seething mass of people, coming and going, all intent upon their various activities. High in the sky, Nanautzin—the Sun—told them it was midday. As they looked up, they only saw a few wisps of clouds, far off, in the enormous blue sky.

This was the day set for the Great Gathering of the People. The festivities would last for several days and perhaps even weeks, as people from far away had come to participate in the Peace Ceremony. Preparations had been going on for three months after Eagle and Deer returned from their mission.

Foods were gathered and stored, temporary housing was constructed, and the baths filled with water to accommodate the multitude. Musicians, dancers, and singers practiced their arts daily. Craftspeople had been working day and night to create items to be used and purchased by the visitors.

The Priestess and the Queen had studied the astrological signs before Eagle and Deer set out on the journey. They had to make sure the aspects were favorable. Now, they stood at the top of the stairs and saw the result of all the preparations. The buildings sparkled in the bright sunlight. Gardens provided shade for the babies and the elderly. Fountains flowed and flowers bloomed. The marketplace was full of vendors, craftspeople, and shoppers. They could hear music and the laughter of the children in the plaza. They could smell the aroma of cooked food. They were satisfied—the City of the Door had opened to its guests and all was well.

They would not greet the visitors on this first day, while they were becoming acclimated to the wonders of the new city; but, on the following morning, they would formally welcome everyone.

They slowly descended the steps to the people waiting below. For those gathered on the plaza, it was a mystical sight. The two Enlightened Leaders, in their most beautiful ceremonial dress, the shimmering shifts made from the fabric their beloved Trader had given them, changed color in the sunlight as they walked down the steps. The shifts were accented with emerald, turquoise and gold jewelry that vied with the blue and green feathers of their headdresses. The jewelry had been gathered quickly from the cavern where Mockingbird had been imprisoned. They were only able to carry a small amount, having to leave most behind as the water rose to cover it. Luckily, they were able to salvage enough to offer as gifts to the heads of the villages and cities that were attending this celebration and ceremony.

The crowd gasped at the sight of the women as they descended. All of the singers, in every neighboring settlement, had sung the prophecies of their coming. The ancient texts, painted in leather books and carved into stone, foretold this moment. The people gazed with awe at the blue eyes of the Queen and the star on the forehead of the Priestess, and knew this was the beginning of a new day—prophecy had become fact.

At the foot of the steps, the original group of travelers from the Aztec capitol stood at attention, waiting to escort the Leaders to the palace to prepare for the rituals of ceremony that would occur the following day. In the meantime, after the Leaders were in the palace readying themselves with cleansing and prayer, the guests visited old friends, ate the prepared foods, and anticipated the next day's activities. The City was alive as thousands of people walked the plaza and causeways. The Queen had spent months planning and organizing her people to make this the most welcoming event. Nothing, it seemed, was overlooked.

2

Before sunrise the next morning, Mockingbird stood halfway up the temple steps and played her flute. The sound reverberated below on the plaza. The City was in a large bowl formation, the surrounding mountains creating a natural amphitheater, and the music was clear to listeners, even far across the plaza. Everyone stopped to listen to the beautiful throaty tones coming from the Queen's clay flute.

One hundred Dancers of the City appeared in beautiful regalia, dancing in time to the flute and the accompanying drums and harps. The music became louder and the dancers moved fluidly, faster and faster.

Abruptly, the music stopped. The whole city seemed to hold its breath. In her clear voice, Mockingbird called out, "Morning Star, Great Seer and Prophetess, The Anointed, The High Priestess of the One!" She turned gracefully, her arm gracefully lifting behind her to indicate the arrival of the Priestess.

Slowly and softly, the musicians once again began to play. The one hundred dancers swayed gently, slowly moving their feet in time as Morning Star slowly descended the towering stairway. Again, the music gradually increased in speed and loudness, until Morning Star finally reached the step that Mockingbird stood upon. Again, the music abruptly ceased.

Morning Star took Mockingbird's hand in hers and raised them high between them. She called out, "My people, this is my Sister! Our Queen! The Enlightened Queen of the City of the Door between Heaven and Earth!"

Everyone on the Plaza stood respectfully, thrilled by the vision of the Enlightened Leaders, the prophesied sisters who came to bring Light and Wisdom to the world. Not a baby whimpered. Not a person spoke.

Behind the temple, a brilliant star lit the pre-dawn sky—the morning star was brighter than it had ever been! It was an omen that the gods were pleased. All was as it should be.

The Priestess, Morning Star, was a vision in the light of the rising Sun. She seemed to be on fire, so glowing was her aspect as a ray of sunlight peeked through the trees to focus on her. The brilliance of her quetzal colors caught the sunlight, subtly changing hues with her slightest movement. The people gasped in awe as she prayed for a blessing on one and all. When she was finished, she once again took Mockingbird's hand in hers.

In one voice, the Priestess and the Queen called out, "Beloved People! We welcome you to the City of the Door! Together, we will participate in the Oneness Celebration, a symbol of the Oneness of all People and all life! Let the Celebration Begin!"

Silence held for two breaths, and then the cheers burst forth, sounding to the ears of Morning Star and Mockingbird like a loud rushing waterfall. Once again, the City moved. The dancers fanned out, creating a walkway for the Enlightened Leaders. As their feet touched the last step, their regally attired mates met them. The four proceeded into the plaza, where the Leaders were escorted to high seats prepared for them by their artisans. There, they awaited the visitors who wished to speak to them.

A long line formed, villagers waiting in their finest clothing, carrying gifts for the Queen and the Priestess. As each got to the front of the line and thanked the Leaders for this wonderful celebration, they offered their gifts. They spoke of what they hoped for in the joining of the people. In turn, Mockingbird and Morning Star thanked the visitors for honoring them with their presence. Then Eagle and

Doorway Series:
Morning Star Rises

Snake offered each a precious gift from the hidden cavern as a sign of friendship.

The people shifted on their feet, wondering what would come next. Never in their lives had they seen so many people together in one place. Never before had they seen such splendor. City residents maneuvered through the throngs, suggesting things of interest for the visitors. Soon, groups of people went their various ways, eager to experience all the wondrous things. Guides took visitors around, explaining what the various buildings were used for. There was the vast library, the various schools, the healing temple, and more.

Vendors passed among the people, selling hot drinks and foods from all the visiting regions as well as the local fare. In one area, children were involved in races and ball games. In another area, young men competed in various physical endurance trials. Young women gathered with their babies and, in the age-old way, discussed different ways to handle fussiness or illnesses and compared the growth of their children. Scholars held lectures on many subjects. Artists and artisans created their works as onlookers watched. Singers, musicians and dancers from all over held performances. There was something of interest for everyone.

3

Mesquite, Wolf and Zolin were hidden within the masses—just a few among the many. No one noticed them, other than to take a wide berth if they happened to come too close. Others seemed to feel discomfort in their presence. It was as if a shroud of gloom hung about them, reaching out to pull them in.

Mesquite's followers milled about, too. They kept a little distance from their leader, but always had her within sight. They had been told to wait for a signal, and their actions had been pre-planned and laid out with great detail; but, the unexpected size of the gathering made Mesquite nervous. She had no idea that so many would come to this place. She tried to convince herself that this was good, because there would be even less likelihood that they would be noticed. The interlopers were in the process of creating a huge following, and she had to stop it. She had made a pact with an insider, one who would never be suspected. They were to meet tonight, by the temple of healing. She was determined to put an end to this reign.

***

Deer and Flower turned from the temple to check on Jaguar. After the ceremony this morning, he had darted off to join the boys in the competitions. He loved to run, and was faster than many of the older boys. He had been talking about the races for days.

"Can you see our son, Husband?" Flower felt the same anxiety in her chest that had been with her since the time she witnessed the jaguar with its mouth surrounding her son's head as it pulled him from the water. At that time, she had felt a cold slice of fear, and then she screamed.

Suddenly, she saw the jaguar run off, leaving her son on the shore. She had thought he was dead; but the jaguar had carried him gently, leaving him none the worse for the experience. Since that time, several years before, she felt that same cold knife slice into her every time she lost sight of her son.

Deer looked about; but, the large numbers of people present would have made it impossible to see the young boy. Knowing his wife's constant worry about Jaguar, he pointed and said, "I think he is over that way, where the boys are having races. Let's go find him. We can watch him run."

Forcing herself to calm down, Flower followed her husband through the throng of people, feeling guilty about her fear. As a follower of the One, she knew that she shouldn't feel that way; but, as a mother, she couldn't help herself. Jaguar was her only child, and he was special. She knew that he had a great destiny if he followed the path, but she still worried.

Deer put his hand on the small of Flower's back, and led her through the crowd. *It would be easy to lose her among all these people,* he thought.

They squeezed through a throng of mountain people wrapped in their colorful blankets, past a group of fishermen and their families, and past a group from the flat open country. Many of these people remembered him from his journey with Eagle. He welcomed them and thanked them for coming, and had to take time to converse with them. He introduced them to Flower, much to her discomfort. She was polite, and asked after their health even though she had only one thing on her mind—and that was to find her son.

She became more and more uneasy as they slowly made their way toward where the younger boys were racing. It was difficult for her to keep her composure and be the welcoming city dweller that she naturally was. She didn't say anything to Deer about her growing dread, because she felt it was just an extension of her childhood trauma when she had been given to the Priesthood of the sun god. It was something she had worked hard to get over, and had felt safe and secure with her good husband and her beautiful child. Now, the numbing fear and dread of the unknown future seemed to well up in her, threatening to drown her in its magnitude.

Deer stopped to buy food from a vendor, warm corn cakes filled with meat and peppers. He knew this was a favorite of Flower's and he wanted her to know how proud he was of her, and how much he valued her.

With a small forced smile, Flower took the offering, and thanked her husband. She tried to nibble at the corn cake, but she had no appetite. Her stomach was in knots from the growing fear that she couldn't shake.

She told herself, I'm imagining things. It's probably the large number of people here. It's bringing back memories of my birth city and the pain I suffered there.

Deer, ever watchful of his sensitive wife, noticed her difficulties. He tried to cheer her up as they walked, telling her stories of his journey to outlying villages with Eagle. He was a good storyteller, but she still couldn't get her mind off her son, and she couldn't chase away the fear.

***

Net and Shell walked the plaza together. Turtle's death had taken a toll on Net, but he was slowly learning to find simple pleasures in life again. His father had been his focus for so long, and he felt the loss deeply. Shell was sensitive to his loss and grief, so she was patient.

Magnolia and Feather walked behind them. The Queen's daughter was having a wonderful time. She feasted on treats from the vendors and kept up a constant chatter about all the fascinating people and their different costumes. When they passed a vendor selling necklaces from the sea, she became ecstatic. She picked up one after the other holding them against her shift.

Then she spied a jade pendant on a thong. "Oh!" she cried, picking it up with reverence. "Oh, it is perfect!" she sighed. "Please Magnolia; I must have this for Shell. Can you tell the vendor that my parents will pay for it?"

Magnolia, pleased with the child's selflessness, explained to the vendor to whom the child belonged. The deal was made, and Feather could barely contain her joy. She thanked the vendor and sprinted ahead to catch up with Shell and Net.

Catching up with the pair, Feather tugged at Shell's arm. "Please, Auntie, bend down so I can tell you something!"

Shell squatted down to eye level with Feather. She looked into the sparkling blue eyes with love and said with a soft smile, "What is it, Little Woman?"

Putting the thong over Shell's head, Feather said gravely, "This is for you, Auntie. It is to remind you that Net will always come back to you."

***

Jaguar saw the strange looking woman with the bone necklace when he was on his way to the area where the boys were racing. He had the feeling that she was watching him; and it gave him an eerie sensation. He told himself it was just the bone necklace. He didn't like the looks of that at all. He saw, too, the fat man with her, but the man didn't give him the same feeling. He just gave Jaguar a feeling of sadness. Then, he noticed another, younger, man talking with the woman. He looked a lot like the woman. He was angular and his eyes were so close together that he looked strange, almost as if he was frowning when he wasn't. Jaguar saw by their clothing and hairstyles that they were from a fishing village. Jaguar wondered if Net knew these people. But, there were people from a lot of villages here, so he dismissed the idea.

He was close now to the racers, so he turned his attention to finding the boys his age. The younger boys would just do sprints—short little footraces here on the edge of the city. But the older boys, like Jaguar, would race long distance, out into the countryside and through many difficult areas. It was a test of endurance and bravery; and Jaguar, almost nine years old, knew he was up to it.

He glanced around to see if any of his friends were there yet. He saw children he didn't know—there must have been fifty boys from ten to twelve years old. They were all older than he was, but he wasn't worried.

A man of the City explained the rules. The route was marked, and it would take them through many difficult areas, but men were waiting at various places to make sure everyone was on the right trail. Every few yards they should look for a red marker. The race would be in the morning, after the Ceremony of Morning Star.

The boys were all excited as they left the area. Jaguar was talking to a boy from a mountain village when his parents found him. After saying goodbye to his new friend, Jaguar walked home with Deer and Flower. He wanted to get a good sleep before the race.

4

Morning Star had spent all day in the Plaza, greeting visitors along with Mockingbird. Still, she wasn't tired. The exhilaration of the morning was still with her. All of the visiting shamans, priests and priestesses, astrologers, and healers from the outlying villages and settlements were invited to spend several days with her and Snake. A large seminar was planned, and it would be an exchange of ideas, beliefs, and visions between all of the nations present.

Mockingbird, too, had planned an exchange of ideas with all the other leaders. She and Eagle would host a huge gathering to discuss the philosophy of law and the intricacies of leading a people, whether it consisted of hundreds or thousands of souls.

These gatherings were an effort to find common ground, and unite all of the people under the same basic tenets so that no fighting or disagreements would splinter them apart. The concept was one of rule through rightness and respect for the individual while integrating the good of all the people. It wasn't based on fear or power, but on the power of the One.

Scribes would be at both meetings, keeping track of all that was discussed, and what the consensus was. Every participant would be allowed whatever time he or she deemed necessary to speak. The civic leaders would meet in the Temple of Education and the spiritual leaders would meet in the Temple of Healing.

But, for tonight, Morning Star and Mockingbird would be by themselves, praying and preparing for the morrow.

***

"What did you mean by what you said to Shell?"

Magnolia was always amazed by this child she had delivered into the world.

"What did you mean when you told Shell the necklace was to remind her that Net would always return?"

They were on their way back to the palace after a full day of enjoying the start of the celebration. Magnolia was exhausted, but Feather was almost as lively as when they started out in the morning.

Feather stopped and looked as if she was trying to remember. "Oh, I know," she said. "Net is going to go away for awhile. But he will come back."

"What do you mean? Where is he going?"

"He is going far away."

Magnolia just shook her head at the little girl. *Such an imagination!* Then, Magnolia remembered that Feather was of the blood of Mockingbird, and she wondered briefly if the tiny girl was able to foretell the future. Magnolia's mind didn't dwell on this. She was so tired from the long day that she only wanted to get the child to bed so she could sleep, too.

She took Feather inside the palace and turned her over to her nurse with a kiss. From there, Magnolia went to the bed she had been assigned. Shell wasn't back yet. Magnolia hoped her niece wouldn't stay out too late, but she knew how exciting it all was to her. She was walking with Net, and she had the energy of youth to keep her interest alive in all there was to see and experience.

She readied herself for sleep and lay down on her bed. Her last thoughts before drifting off to sleep were about Shell. Her sister's daughter was like her own. Shell's mother died in childbirth, and Magnolia had been present as midwife. She still felt guilty that she hadn't been able to save her sister's life. As she lay bleeding to death, Magnolia made a vow that she would raise Shell as her own. She swore that she would always keep her safe.

***

Mesquite and her followers had heard enough. They left the city, a few at a time, to meet in their camp. She had met with the insider by the Temple of Healing. Now, she just needed to get her followers organized and the plan would proceed.

5

In the forest, a gigantic tree was blessed by the Shaman, and felled. A large group of men carried the tree to the city, making sure not to let it touch the ground. It was carried to the plaza in front of the highest temple, the Temple of Quetzalcoatl. There, it was stripped of its bark and branches. Vines were wrapped around it, and they raised the tree to standing position. It was secured into the ground.

People of the City and all of the visitors gathered in the predawn for the Ceremony of Quetzalcoatl. They had bathed in the City's wondrous bathhouses. They had dressed in their finest celebration clothing. Then, they waited in anticipation.

The Morning Star, the Heart of Quetzalcoatl, shone brightly in the predawn sky. The sun slowly rose behind the temple. Still the light of the Morning Star was visible.

From the apex of the temple, a flute is heard, playing a sweet throaty melody. Then, from below on the plaza, flutes and drums joined in. Dancers entered the area, performing a beautiful dance in time to the music. The music and dance became more and more intense, lifting the vibrations of the watchers. They swayed and chanted in rhythm with the music. Their feathered costumes and jewelry swayed and tinkled, adding to the harmony. Everything stopped. It was totally still and quiet.

From high on the temple, a pure voice began to sing softly, and all listened carefully to hear the words:

Doorway Series:
Morning Star Rises

The Tree Of Life grows
In the Land of Mystery:
There we were created;
There we were born.
There He by whom all things live
Spins the thread of our lives.[4]

Five Flyers came forth from the base of the temple—five young men in feathered costumes—appearing as birds. They carried thongs as they shinnied up the pole to the platform on top. One attached his thong to the hub of the pole and wrapped it around and around the pole, then wrapped the other end around his waist. One by one, each Flyer did this. Then, one by one, they fell backwards off the platform. Soon all five were soaring gently around the pole, lower and lower, resembling the birds they imitated.

The voice from on high became louder and clearer:

You have become the Tree of Life.
Dying, you have been born again.
Swaying, you spread your branches
And stand before the Giver of all life.
In your boughs our home shall be:
We will be your flowers.[5]

The first to upright himself and land gently with his feet on the ground was Net. Shell watched with a feeling she didn't understand. It was beautiful, seeing the Flyers soar through the air, honoring the Great Quetzalcoatl, the giver of law, culture, and knowledge. She was so proud of Net, as comfortable in the air as he was in the sea. It took great courage—and more—to fall from the high platform. Still, she had what she could only describe as a feeling of loneliness and she didn't know why. If it weren't for the Ceremony, she would go to Morning Star and ask her what was causing this dis-ease in her; but the Priestess would be busy from morning until night for days.

* * *

The Priestess had ended her song of prayer to the One God. A hush fell over the crowd. The rising sun cast red and gold over the plaza, and the temple itself was washed in gold, looking as if it was on fire, as Morning Star once again walked up to the top of the stairs to stand beside Mockingbird. They stood for a few minutes, looking over the city, before they disappeared into the structure at the top of the high temple.

Magnolia turned to Shell, and seeing her distress, whispered to her, "My daughter, what is it that disturbs you so greatly? Is there a problem between you and Net? Or were you frightened for him?"

Shell clutched the jade dolphin that hung from a necklace around her neck. "No, Auntie. I was not frightened when he flew around the Tree of Life. My fear is of something else, but I don't know what. It seems silly, I know, but I have felt unease since yesterday. I don't know why, Auntie. I feel that Net will be leaving me and I may never see him again!"

Suddenly, the words of Feather echoed in Magnolia's mind. She remembered the little girl's prophecy of the night before.

6

Morning Star and Mockingbird sat in meditation inside the apex of the pyramid as the city went about its celebration below. This was where they did their meditation every morning, putting aside the cares of the day, to join with their higher guidance. It was the most sacred spot on earth, where the veil between the earth and the heavens was the thinnest. The women were adepts in the mysteries, having been raised in a temple and trained daily by their old Priestess, Tlacotl.

As they drew in the light through the crown of their heads, they were simultaneously transported to a different time and place. The feeling of Oneness enfolded them, swirling visions surrounded them, and a brilliant light warmed their souls. They found themselves in a familiar place—a crystal temple where they were surrounded by the warm light, music of the stars, and an intense feeling of joy not possible on the earth.

Suddenly they were witnessing an event that had not yet happened on earth—something that firmed their resolution to work toward unifying the people down in the plaza.

***

In the bustling city, it wasn't apparent that anything had changed. All of the events moved forward as planned.

In the Temple of Education, Mockingbird stood regally before the assembly. Magnificent in her bearing, blue eyes on fire, Mockingbird spoke to the rulers and leaders of the various lands of the vision she and Morning Star had long shared, and how the Celebration of Oneness would cement the friendship and unity of all the tribes—all the villages and cities. They spoke of law and justice and right. They shared their experiences and talked about what had worked well for them and what had not. They recognized in Mockingbird the fire of the law of One.

In the Temple of Healing, Morning Star stood amongst the prophets, seers, healers, shamans, priests and priestesses. She spoke to them of the vision she and Mockingbird shared. She told them of the long journey her family had made and of the strange and wondrous events they had experienced. She told them of the guidance and direction they received from the Great Quetzalcoatl because they followed the laws of the One. They witnessed the light surrounding her, witnessed the star on her forehead, and witnessed the powers of her truth.

In the City of the Door between Heaven and Earth, the city that followed the ways and laws of the One God of Duality, the One God in Two Forms, as taught by the Great Prince Quetzalcoatl, the Feathered Serpent and Divine Twin, the Enlightened Leaders in their duality show the people the way to Enlightenment.

In the Plaza, amongst all of the people from the different parts of the land, Singers wove their way through the crowds and sang the message:

There are those who guide us,
They govern us, they carry us on their backs...
Those who receive the name Quetzalcoatl...
They lead us, they guide us, they tell us the way[6]

As the people's spirits and vibrations increased and rose, a tangible luminescence was seen and felt in the air. The animal world, watching from the trees, air and land were witness to the glow emanating from the city.

7

Feather laughed happily at the antics of Snake. A magnificent storyteller, he was able to add so much to his words with gestures and postures. He was her favorite uncle and she was happiest when she could spend time with him. For all of his wisdom, he was childlike in his joy. He loved to play and laugh and to teach the children. They were comfortable with him because they could sense his goodness.

Snake was an enigma to some. They had grown up surrounded by an air of defeat, of pre-destination. They felt as though they were born, suffered, and died, and nothing they did really made a change in their lives. Snake always looked for the positive, and didn't waste time or energy thinking negatively. He knew that he made his own life, and that when things seemed to be dark it was only because he lived in a world of shadow.

Now, they were going to watch the start of Jaguar's race. They wouldn't be able to see the whole thing because it was out into the country and forest, and they couldn't keep up with the racers. They would see the beginning and the end, Uncle had told her.

"There he is, Uncle! There is Jaguar!" Feather jumped up in down while pointing to her hero, her exuberant display attracting the attention and fond smiles of people nearby. She was known everywhere she went by the flashing blue eyes in the little round face.

"Ah, Jaguar!" Snake honored Jaguar with his wide happy grin and a wave of his strong brown hand.

Hearing the voice of Snake, Jaguar glanced over the many boys into the crowd beyond. His heart filled with pride when he saw Uncle and Feather. He tried hard to appear grown up and dignified, but a small smile played with the corners of his brown eyes. Then he caught sight of his parents, Deer and Flower, coming up just behind Snake. His heart swelled at the sight.

The boys were eager to begin, their adrenalin pumping through their veins. Jaguar turned his attention back to the race starter. At the first sound of the conch shell, the race was on. With a great roar, the assembled crowd cheered them on.

***

At a checkpoint in the forest, Net waited for the arrival of the first racers. He took a drink of water from his flask and munched on berries from a nearby bush. It would be a long day, but soon the boys would begin to come by, and there should be a steady stream of them after that.

He heard a sound behind him, and as he began to turn, he felt a sharp pain in his head, and all went black. He didn't feel the rough hands pulling him along the ground, the dead wood on the forest floor tearing at his skin, or the vines roughly binding his arms and legs together.

***

Shell's face paled under her black hair, making her dark eyes look even larger than usual. With one hand she clutched at the dolphin on the end of her necklace. With the other, she clutched at Magnolia just as her knees buckled.

Alarmed, Magnolia grasped her by the waist, holding her upright.

"What is it, Child? Are you ill?"

Faintly, Shell answered, "I don't know, Auntie. My head hurts and I feel sick in my stomach."

Magnolia's first thought was that Shell was pregnant. If she was, it was Net's baby, and that would be good, because they loved each other.

Deer and Snake saw Magnolia's distress over her niece, and Deer carried Shell back to the palace. Feather followed with the nurse and baby. They created quite a stir—some people who saw them voiced concern and some smiled knowingly, thinking along the same lines as Magnolia.

8

Zolin finished tying Net with the vines, stood, and looked him over. He wasn't too sure his mother had a good idea here, but he didn't dare to defy her. She had spent a good share of his life telling him that he was the heir to his grandfather, Ollin. She had fed him stories of the evils of Mockingbird and her followers along with his breast milk. Still, he couldn't help but believe that the Aztec interlopers had a more powerful god than his mother did. Why else would his grandfather have been defeated by them?

Zolin was awkward and ungainly but he wasn't stupid by any means. As a child he had felt embarrassed when his mother taunted the other boys when they were trying to be helpful to him. He knew his shortcomings, but he also had a tendency to like the feeling of superiority instilled by his mother. She often told him that he had his grandfather's intelligence and her looks. He didn't know that Wolf was actually his half-brother and Ollin his real father; but he sometimes mused about how strange it was that his father could pass down a good mind when it was so clearly lacking in him. His mother told him that Wolf took after his own mother who wasn't very clever, but that the gods had allowed him to carry the intelligence in his seed, if not in his head.

"What do you want me to do with him now?" Zolin asked.

"Bring him back to camp," she answered. "No, on second thought, these two can carry him!" She pointed at two of her followers.

Disgruntled, they picked him up, one on each end, and followed a smug Zolin through the trees.

Doorway Series:
Morning Star Rises

***

In the palace, Shell rested uncomfortably. She reclined on a bed, back cushions propping her partially upright, but she was embarrassed to have caused such a scene. Snake had just finished checking her out, and he found nothing wrong. He thought she might be pregnant, but it was too early to tell. He told her to stay where she was and rest. Magnolia was skilled in nursing, and she would care for her.

Shell was still slightly agitated, feeling that something was wrong and at the same time not knowing what it could be. The pain in her head had been swift and severe, but lasted only a short time. Then she had felt sick to her stomach and dizzy. Now, she was numb, as if her body was asleep.

The baby's nurse had put him down for a nap, but Feather stayed with Shell and Magnolia. She felt something gnawing at her consciousness, just out of reach. Suddenly, she jumped up from the floor where she had been sitting.

"I know what it is!"

The two women looked at Feather with confusion.

"What do you mean, Little Woman?" Magnolia asked, suddenly afraid of the answer.

"I know why Auntie Shell became ill!"

Magnolia held out her hand and said, "Come, Feather! Do not distress your Auntie! Come with me to see if the baby boy sleeps. He may want you to sing to him!"

She hurried Flower out of the room.

***

Fifty-three boys waited for the race to begin. Jaguar wasn't in the front when the racers set out. He ran at a steady pace, knowing he needed to conserve his energy. He moved effortlessly in this beginning leg of the race, watching for the red markers and going over the map in his mind. This was the same route he had taken months ago when he had followed Mother Jaguar's call to help Feather. He listened, now, for the large cat, but didn't hear her.

The boys all wore only breechclouts and various forms of footwear. Some were tattooed all over their bodies and some were painted with symbols to bring them luck and protection. This was a big event, and the families of the boys would be waiting at the finish line to welcome them back with much cheering and praise.

There was some wagering going on over who would win, but Jaguar knew his family wouldn't be involved in that. He was always taught to do the best he could, and that would be honor enough. Still, he hoped he would do well and make his family proud.

The forested area around the city was well traveled and the paths were wide. Two boys passed Jaguar as he maintained his steady pace. He wasn't concerned, because he knew a steady pace could win the race.

He breathed with ease, taking in the heady smell of the jungle, listening to the colorful birds, watching out for poisonous snakes, dodging the fruits being hurled by the howler monkeys, and making sure he didn't step into any holes that could twist his ankle. It was a fine day for the race, the sun warming his skin as it peeked through the high roof of the forest here and there. He stopped at the first checkpoint and, barely pausing, took a sip of the water provided by the man who waited there. He was pointed in the right direction, and continued his easy pace.

As he ran toward the open area beyond, he thought he heard it—the barely perceptible sound of Mother Jaguar in his head. He listened closely, but he didn't hear it again.

9

Eagle and Deer stood looking through a window of the palace at the horde of people below in their beautiful plaza. They had posted men around the city as peacekeepers, in case of any trouble.

"Everything seems to be going well," Deer commented.

Eagle said, "We haven't had any serious problems, yet. Yaotl reported to me that Wolf and Mesquite were seen leaving the city this morning."

"And the meeting?"

"It went according to plan."

"Good."

***

In both the Temple of Education and the Temple of Healing, the groups took a break. They wandered out onto the plaza where many vendors were ready to offer their various foods. The odors of the foods commingled in the air with the heady scent of the jungle flowers.

Sighting Morning Star, Mockingbird caught her attention and the two met up over a table laden with corn and meat dishes, fresh fruits, nuts and honey sweetened treats.

Mockingbird asked, "Ah, Little Sister, how did your morning go?"

Morning Star smiled at the nickname. "Very well, Older Sister. And yours?"

"Very well, indeed. We are coming to an understanding and agreement and are learning much from each other."

Vendors approached them with a great show of respect. The pair bought their favorite foods, and went to sit on a bench by the nearest fountain. The water, jetting high in the air, drifted in a light mist on the gentle breeze, cooling the air. The sun shone high overhead in a clear blue sky, hummingbirds hovered and fed on the nectar of the vast flowering gardens, and dancers performed nearby to the gentle music of flutes and harps.

As they chatted, they saw Flower approaching from a distance.

"She's here," Mockingbird said gravely.

Morning Star asked, "Are you going to talk to her about it?"

Rising from her seat, Mockingbird said, "Perhaps we should take her to a private place, Star."

***

When they were out of hearing range, Magnolia turned Feather around and squatted down to her level.

"Now tell me, Little One. What did you mean by saying that you knew what had caused Shell to be ill?"

"I saw what happened, Auntie. I saw what happened to Net. Auntie Shell's head was hurting because she could feel it when the man hit Net on the head."

Feather seemed very matter-of-fact about what she reported; but Magnolia was stunned.

She demanded, "How did you see this, Feather?"

"I just saw it, Auntie."

"But how? Did this happen in the city?"

"No, Auntie. It happened by some trees. When Shell became ill, I saw the man hit Net on his head!"

***

"This isn't what we had planned, Mother! How is this going to help to bring those women to their knees? This man isn't even related to them!"

Zolin was beginning to think his mother was losing her wits. She was acting irrationally, and not following her plan.

Mesquite snapped, "I know what I'm doing! That woman—Flower—she is the wife of the Consort's right hand man! She said she could bring us great wealth. She said that she could sneak you into the hidden vault of riches under the temples. But I don't trust her! We need something to force her to cooperate. If we keep the hostage, she will not try to trick us!"

Zolin gave this some thought. "As wise as you are, Mother, I think we could use someone else to our advantage. The boy, Jaguar...I have heard he is racing today. If we send some of the men to intercept him, his mother will never refuse us. He is her only son and I hear that she is very fond of him. She would not dare to betray us if we hold him."

10

Now, in the jungle again, Jaguar ran alone. He didn't see any of the other boys. A whisper entered his mind, almost a howl, almost a plea. It was Mother Jaguar, he was sure. He saw pictures in his head as he ran. It was as if he was looking through the large cat's eyes, seeing what she saw from ground level. Rats and mice scurried through the underbrush, a flying squirrel dropped right before her, causing a rumble in her stomach. Toucans and howler monkeys floated in his vision as Mother Jaguar climbed up a fallen tree and jumped onto a low branch. Every slight movement caught her eye and was processed in her mind, and Jaguar witnessed it all.

As much as he wanted to race, the call of the Mother Jaguar was stronger. She had saved him from danger, had helped him to save Feather, and he had to answer her call. He stopped and listened, hoping to get a direction, but now the cat was silent. He went on, his pace steady, the rhythm working to put him into a place where he could hear more clearly.

Now, he saw her—the Mother Jaguar stood on a branch, her tawny velvet fur spotted with black designs, her muscular body taut and her mouth open, calling to him.

He turned off the trail, knowing, without knowing how, the right direction to take. His feet, in tune with the rain forest, knew just where to step without his guidance. The large leaves, broken wood, scurrying noises, and pungent scents of which he was semi-aware with his five senses were overlaid with the sights and sounds experienced by the Mother Jaguar. It would have been a strange and disorienting experience, but his lifetime of being Jaguar had made it normal for him.

He could see her now, reflected in the sunlit water of the lake, her green eyes staring back from the shimmering water. He felt her focus, watching through the surface reflection and deep into the water, the small striped fish darting here and there among the driftwood and weeds. Then, she threw back her head, closed her eyes and roared.

***

The three women stood in the innermost portion of the temple, surrounded by wall carvings and statues of many gods. The Priestess Morning Star, the Queen Mockingbird, and Flower, the mother of Jaguar, gathered to share very important business. Shortly after they met, Eagle, Deer, and Snake arrived.

Flower's voice trembled as she related what had happened that morning. She had met with Mesquite as planned. Word had been spread about that Flower was jealous of Morning Star and Mockingbird, and would be eager for the downfall of the Enlightened Rulers. Mesquite heard about it and was quick to take advantage of the trouble she thought was brewing among the royal family in the new city. Being who she was, she had no difficulty in believing that Flower's jealousy could lead her to betray her leaders and friends. She had arranged, through messengers, to meet with Flower and to set up a plan.

***

Flower was terrified, but she was determined to overcome her fear. Finally, she could be of some help to those who had given her a new life. She had left the Aztec city because she had nothing there to hold onto, and because her husband wanted to go with these women whom the prophets had decreed were the Enlightened Rulers. She went because her husband and her son were her only security and strength. But something happened on the long journey. She grew to love the women, Mockingbird and

Star, and she heard their truth and she knew it was her truth, too. A cord of familiarity was struck in her deepest being and she recognized what she had long known on another hidden level. She would gladly die a thousand deaths rather than betray them.

Flower knew that nothing occurred by accident—that a great plan had been behind her connection to the leaders of her new home. When she had been given to the temple on the same day as they were, way back when they were children, it was because she belonged to their soul group—a group of beings who had planned to incarnate in that place at the same time so they could fulfill this prophecy.

Flower thought about her son, Jaguar, who was such a gentle soul, but one with so much promise. He was filled with such love for the creatures of the earth that he had been adopted by the mightiest cat in the jungle—the Mother Jaguar. Many war societies adopted the jaguar as a god, but this creature knew her son as a shaman and bowed to his wisdom. Flower loved her boy with a fiery passion, and wanted him to live in a society where he could reach his highest potential. This, too, gave her the strength to face Mesquite and to play her part in making and keeping the City of the Door such a society.

***

Eager to hear how the meeting went, Mockingbird asked: "Tell us, Flower, did the woman, Mesquite come as planned?"

"Yes, my Queen."

Just as Flower began to tell them what had occurred, Magnolia begged to be allowed entrance. She trembled, her face paled, and she stumbled over her words in her haste to relay what she had learned.

"My Queen, Seer, Lady," she said as she nodded to each woman. "Please...oh...forgive this intrusion, but I have news of vital importance!"

Mockingbird, shocked by Magnolia's pallor said, "Speak, Lady."

"It is Feather. She saw something in a vision. She said she saw someone hit Net over the head!"

As the words tumbled from Magnolia's lips, Morning Star began to see what she was describing. She said, "I, too, see this happening, and more. I see Zolin tying Net with vines. He is lying on the ground of the forest. I can see others there. Two men are carrying him, but I am not sure where they are."

Mockingbird said to Flower, "What did Mesquite say about the plan to show Zolin the cavern of jewels?"

"My Queen, she said that she wanted him to have escorts. She agreed to have Zolin and two other men meet me when the sun goes down. I insisted, Lady, as you suggested, that he come alone, but she would have no part of that. She said that she wasn't a fool, and that Zolin would meet me at sunset with two of his men, and if I didn't agree to that, she would find a way to make sure that I did."

Eagle said, "The woman is obviously dangerous. She must have quite a following to dare the capture of a friend of the Queen. We must go after her."

Then, the Shaman spoke, "Consort, let me see if I can find out where they camp and how many there are. Perhaps we can free Net with no loss of life."

He sat down on the floor and within seconds, he closed his eyes and breathed so slowly that the rest weren't sure if he was breathing at all. As Morning Star watched, she saw his spirit lift from his body, a white light rising. Soon, all she could see was a fine golden cord coming from the top of his head and extending high above.

***

There! There is Net. He is still unconscious. I will try to talk to him. Net, hear me. I am here. We are coming to release you.

Doorway Series:
Morning Star Rises

What has happened, Shaman?
You have been hit on the head and taken prisoner.
Your body is not conscious. I can see that there is no
permanent damage. We will be back soon to release you.
You are not alone, Net. We are here for you. There, I have
helped your healing. Sleep now. Sleep and heal.

Snake opened his eyes and said, "I have seen Net."

11

Net found himself face down on the ground, his hands bound behind him and his feet tied together. There was no escape. His throat was sore from dryness, and insects crawled over his bruised body. Spitting dirt from his mouth, he tried to see if anyone was near him. He tried to lift his head, but he winced from the sharp pain of having been tied in this position for so long.

He heard two men talking off to his right. "Ah, look at this big one! We will have fresh fish to eat! It isn't ocean fish, but it will do!"

Net's face was turned away from the voice, and he didn't want to draw attention to himself yet. He waited, hoping there would be more talking. He didn't have to wait long.

"Ho!" Net heard a second voice. He could hear the men splashing in the water. They must be near the lake east of the City. It was a good fishing lake, when one was away from the Village—not the sea, but a good lake.

"Ho!" Again he heard the voice. "My fish is much larger than yours! What a fisherman I am! Ayah, I am great!" The man chuckled.

Net felt that he should know the two voices. He hoped they would keep up the banter so he could be sure.

"Where are the Priestess and her shadow?" The first man asked, referring to Mesquite and Zolin.

"They are gone to the City. If we are lucky, they will be gone for a long time!" The second man laughed again.

The first man warned, "You had best be careful what you say, Cocom! The forest has ears! And you know

Mesquite is very powerful! Your words could be your undoing!"

Just then, a jaguar roar was heard in the forest.

Cocom said nervously, "You know I jest, Pacal! I just meant it would be good to surprise our Priestess with some good fresh fish!"

Net realized he knew these two men. They were from his village—outcasts of a sort, who followed Mesquite because they believed she was powerful. They weren't evil men, just inclined to be lazy and more than ready to let someone else do their thinking.

He thought, *I wonder if I can talk them into letting me go.*

Net's pretense of still being unconscious worked, and he heard Cocom say, "The fish boy is still out. I wonder what Mesquite plans to do with him?"

Pacal said, "She will probably offer him to her god of death."

Cocom, horrified, exclaimed, "But I have known him since he was born! Surely you will not be a party to such a thing?"

"Oh, you are such a fool, Cocom. Do you not know when I am making a joke?"

"What if this is her plan?"

Turning his face from Cocom, Pacal didn't answer.

From the jungle, the voice of the jaguar roared again. She sounded closer.

***

The original band of travelers from the Aztec capitol, now the leaders of the City of the Door, waited as Snake sent his spirit out to search for Net. Everyone present prayed earnestly as they watched the light expand around his body. At last, they noticed he was back. He opened his eyes and took a deep breath. In silent support, they waited for him to speak about what he had learned.

"Net lives," he said softly. "He is unconscious, but his body will survive. He is bound with vines. He is at a place you know—the lake west of the City where we sometimes fish."

"Did you see anyone else?" Eagle asked.

"I saw some others there," Snake replied. "Two men were spearing fish in the lake. Others milled about, but didn't seem to have much purpose. I counted twenty-four including the two fishing. Net was lying face down on the ground, but no one was near him."

Deer asked, "Did you see Mesquite or Zolin?"

"No," the Shaman replied. "But, then, I wasn't looking for them. I didn't see Mesquite's husband, Wolf, either."

He added, "Usually, when I do this, I am instantly at the side of the person I am looking for, and I don't see anything else. This time, I told myself to look around so that we would know where he was. I saw the men, but not Mesquite, her husband, or her son."

Magnolia asked, "Was he hurt? Could you tell?"

"He had a bump on his head. His spirit pulled out of his body for a time to get away from the pain. It was as if his spirit was sleeping, and I had to wake it up to talk to him."

Magnolia said, "Net has been like a son to me since his mother died. And now his father is gone, too. My niece, Shell, loves him. Please tell me he will be all right."

The Shaman replied thoughtfully, "I did heal him, but his injuries weren't too serious. He will recover. The main problem is getting him away from that camp by the lake. We must find a way to bring him back here to the City. We must also find a way to do it without harming anyone. This is our law, and our way of life. We are people of peace and we are creating a place of love. We cannot build this type of society on the bones of others!"

***

Doorway Series:
Morning Star Rises

Jaguar heard the roar again. The young boy lifted his head, sniffing the air. He was getting close to Mother Jaguar. His child body, lean-muscled and limber, glowed a golden brown when the sun's rays caught his skin through the high forest growth. His black hair, bobbed beneath his ears, moved as he searched through the maze of green.

Jaguar now was tattooed on his chest, back and arms. Symbols of Quetzalcoatl, Jaguar, and the Sun adorned his skin. On both cheeks he was tattooed with the symbol of the calmecac, the school for priests, which he had begun to attend.

Spotting a large boa ahead of him, he talked to it in his mind.

"Mighty Boa, I am following Mother Jaguar."

The snake, fat and glossy, hung from the tree above the path, staring directly at Jaguar. The snake pulled up, clearing Jaguar's path.

Jaguar had no fear of the rainforest or its inhabitants. He was one with the jungle just as Net was one with the sea. As he moved on, following the urging he could feel in his body, he heard the call of Mother Jaguar.

12

Zolin followed his mother back toward the city. He had convinced her that the wise thing to do would be to intercept Jaguar on the racing route and use him as leverage to deal with Flower.

Now, he began to have his doubts. The vision of Deer, the soldier father of Jaguar, kept intruding on his thoughts—Deer, the second in command to the mighty warrior, Eagle. Even as far away as Zolin's remote fishing village outside the Aztec Empire, Eagle and Deer were known as skilled warriors. Stories brought by traders and seafarers told of the power of these men; but he had been told, too, that they had received visions from the Great One that caused them to lay down their arms against others.

Zolin was nervous. He had become so used to thinking of these people as peace lovers that he forgot their history. What if a personal threat to one of their own caused them to forget their new ideals? They had a mighty contingent of men at their disposal. Zolin knew that Eagle's men constantly trained with physical endurance and weaponry, even though they were peacekeepers and not warriors. He groaned aloud at the thought of an army of men after their small band.

Mesquite's head whipped to her right when her son groaned. "What is it, Zolin? Why do you groan like an old man?"

"I have remembered the stories about the Soldiers of the City, and am now wondering if we are about to bring death upon ourselves."

"But, Son, these men have lost their might. They are weaklings now, serving a weak god. Love and peace—bah! They are not men any longer! They are no danger to us!"

"Mother, you know many things, but I wonder if you don't forget how protective they are of their women and children. In their worry over their safety, they could forget about their new religion and turn back to the old ways. Aztec Soldiers are nothing to toy with!"

Mesquite mulled this over for a bit, and for the first time, she started to doubt the wisdom of her plan.

***

The gatherings of the wise ones in the temples would begin again on the following morning. For the rest of the day, the Queen and the Priestess were free to mingle with the people or to do what ever they desired. It was set up this way so that the leaders of the other villages and settlements would have time to take part in the festivities. This gave Morning Star and Mockingbird time to deal with the issues threatening the peace of their City. They also wanted to check on their children—to be sure they were safe.

When they arrived at the nursery, Feather ran to her mother. Then she remembered her manners.

"Good day Nantli and Auntie." She bowed gracefully, and then her high spirits took over. She could barely stand still.

"Nantli, may I please go out into the City this day?"

Mockingbird kneeled down to face Feather.

"My only daughter, tell me what you wish to do in the City today," she teased.

"I wish to see everything and do everything!"

"But Daughter, that may not be possible in only one day."

"Then, Nantli, I will go out the next day and the next day and the next until I have done this!"

Doorway Series:
Morning Star Rises

Mockingbird was amused by her child's desire to experience everything, but it concerned her, too. Feather had a thirst for life and for knowledge that appeared unquenchable.

She saw that Feather was dressed in a multi-colored shift, wore a seashell necklace from Shell, and her hair was worn in a simple style. A polished emerald hanging from a gold band adorned the center of her forehead just above her brows.

Beneath the emerald, Feather's blue eyes flashed with anticipation; but she was well mannered enough to wait for her mother's reply.

Mockingbird asked, "Have you studied today?"

"Yes, Nantli. I studied astronomy with Yax Pac, and writing with Ah Cacao. Ah Cacao said that I am getting very good at copying. And, Nantli, there is a new comet in the sky. Yax Pac said that it was seen first one the day before the Celebration began. He said it is a blessing from the One Great God!"

Morning Star was pleased with Feather's interest in her studies. "Little One, you are an excellent student!"

"Thank you, Auntie. Is it true? About the blessing?"

"Yes, Little One. This is what The One God has told me."

Feather seemed to consider Morning Star's answer. Then she said, "Auntie, I sometimes hear a voice. It tells me things. Sometimes others cannot hear it."

Morning Star said, "That is because you listen better than some others can, Feather. You have special ears and eyes. Sometimes you see things that others can't see, too. Can you tell us what you saw happening to Net?"

Feather closed her eyes. "I see him now. He is talking to two men. He is rubbing his head."

She opened her eyes. "I can't see him anymore."

Mockingbird asked, "Feather, think carefully. Did you see where Net is now?"

"Oh, yes, Nantli. He is by a lake with the two men. One of them is cleaning fish."

Feather seemed to be seeing something else. After a second, she said, "Nantli! Auntie! Jaguar is running through the trees."

Morning Star said, "Yes, Little One. He is in the race."

"No, Auntie! He is following the voice of Mother Jaguar!"

**

Eagle and Deer led a small troop of soldiers from the city. They moved swiftly, trying to avoid groups of admirers. The men were impressive in their uniforms—the leaders resplendent in feathered adornments. Tattoos and paintings on the faces and bodies of the men were signs of allegiance and protection from harm. Cotton skirts fell to the top of the knees, and cotton vests filled with rock salt protected them from weapons. Some carried large colorful shields, decorated with the adornments proclaiming them to be followers of Quetzalcoatl—or Kulkulkan, as the locals knew the ancient bringer of civilization.

Eagle wished they could depart without notice, but the City was so filled with people, that it was impossible. Many visitors thought they were parading to show their glory, and gathered around to honor them. Eagle was eager to be out of the city and on the way to the lake to bring Net back.

Net and his father had been indispensable allies when the new rulers arrived from the Aztec Empire. They had taken them into their village, and introduced them to their people. Turtle had recognized Mockingbird and Morning Star as the prophesied Enlightened Leaders who would come to create a City of Peace, dedicated to the One God. The people of the fishing village had also recognized them and honored them—all except the Shaman, Ollin.

Doorway Series:
Morning Star Rises

Now, Ollin was gone, dying from his attempt to destroy the Enlightened Leaders, and their good friend, Turtle, was also gone; but Turtle's son was still alive. He had been taken by Ollin's self-declared replacement, the female Shaman, Mesquite.

Eagle understood that Mesquite was dangerous—dangerous because she was motivated by anger, jealousy and greed. As he thought of this, he stepped into the forest at the edge of the city—and he heard the jaguar roar.

13

Mother Jaguar lived a simple life: hunting when she was hungry, sleeping, mating in season, and sunning herself whenever she could. When she felt the urge to call out to the two-legged boy, she didn't know why. She was compelled by something greater than she was. Now, she felt a stirring in her muscles. Languidly rising from her resting place in the tall grass, she stretched her neck upward, nose sniffing the air. She smelled man. The scent tantalized her, causing her to crouch low, ready to spring. Her spotted tail whipped from side to side, and her muscles twitched. Her ears were alert as well as her eyes and nose. She heard the sound of man-call. There, ahead on the path, a female led several males.

Yes, the female was definitely the leader. The Mother Jaguar could feel the subservience of the males. Spirit moved her and she followed, stalking the movement of the humans. It was more of a game with her than an urge to hunt. It was part of her natural instinct to practice the art of the finding the right moment to pounce. Gradually, she lost interest. Feeling a pull to her boy cub, she raised her head once more and called to him.

Her roar was plaintive, her mind sending out a signal simultaneously with her voice. The humans were dangerous. She wanted her cub by her side.

***

Jaguar's youth was an asset in this type of distance running. His young, supple body had the ability to maintain a steady pace. He breathed easily, loping through the forest like the huge cat he was named for. Around his neck, he wore the stone he had found on one of his trips into the jungle. It seemed to him as though Mother Jaguar had led him to it. One day when he had heeded her call, he found her lying on the grass in the sunlight. She lay stretched out, her tail twitching gently, her front paw batting the stone about. It sparkled in the sun. She languidly pulled her body up and walked a few feet away, turned her massive head, and watched Jaguar as he picked up the stone. It was half the size of his hand, red and translucent. He had asked an artisan to fit it to a thong that he could wear, and its weight on his chest comforted him now. It seemed to snuggle against his brown skin, its warmth giving him energy.

In the back of his mind, he held the thought that he would be in his ninth year soon, no longer a child, but not yet a man. His body was beginning to stretch out, and his mother told him he resembled his father, Deer. He looked down at the long legs stretching out in front, as if they were separate from him, his feet knowing exactly where to land. He was fascinated with his body these days, constantly looking for signs that he was becoming a man.

Manhood was something to look forward to, or so the bigger boys told him. He felt that life was pretty good as it was—but, then, he wasn't as interested in social activities as the other boys were. He was happiest in the jungle with the animals, living life as he had when his parents took him on the long journey.

Suddenly, he saw Mesquite and her men. No, it wasn't quite seeing. It was as if they were there, but not there. Then he realized he was seeing through the eyes of Mother Jaguar.

He heard her again—this time, she was closer. He actually heard her with his ears. He touched the stone on his chest, and it grew warmer. Looking up into the sky overhead, he saw a lone eagle circling.

***

Morning Star led Mockingbird and Snake to the top of the pyramid temple through an inner passageway. She carried an object wrapped in golden cloth. The pyramid was capped with a temple. The three of them entered the temple from inside, but were able to see out onto the plaza below. They could also see the sky, the tops of the trees, the mountains and sea. They had come up here once more to commune with Spirit. This was a place where the veil between heaven and earth was thinnest.

The three sat in a circle, the bundle in the center of the floor between them. Morning Star leaned her graceful back, reaching out with slender well-formed arms, and unwrapped the object. She nodded at Mockingbird, who held her clay flute to her mouth and began to play the soft husky melody that enveloped them and brought a warmth and tingle as energy moved up their spines. Snake held his drum in one hand and beat it slowly with a padded stick until it seemed to echo the heartbeat inside their chests.

The Crystal Skull, resting on the golden cloth, looked amazingly like a human skull, but it was carved in one piece from a large crystal. It had been a perfect crystal, without flaw or discoloration. The First Men had formed the skull out of their wisdom and understanding of the ability of objects to hold power and knowledge. They knew that crystal had special properties—that it was a living form capable of change and regeneration. Shamans and Healers used crystals in their work, using them to soothe and calm, to activate sluggish systems, and to magnify their own healing energies; but the Crystal Skull was much more than this.

Generations of Healers and Priestesses had temporarily possessed the Crystal Skull. It had passed down from woman to woman through the ages, becoming more and more filled with the power of those who had used it. It held information that the Initiated could access and it magnified the abilities of the holder.

Morning Star had received the Skull from her teacher and mentor, Tlacotl, the Aztec Priestess and

Astrologer who had helped Mockingbird and her to escape the rite of sacrifice. She had given it to Morning Star as the rightful holder of the power. It was she who had told Morning Star of her destiny, and it was she who had died to fulfill that destiny. Now, Tlacotl's power was a part of the Crystal Skull, and it was this part that Morning Star called upon to help them.

She prayed to the One God and, already in an altered state of Consciousness, her body a vessel for receiving the truth and enlightenment, she raised her slender arms up high, and called to Tlacotl:

"My Priestess, my Teacher, my Mother, we ask you to come to us now, to help us in our need, as you have said you would. We are dedicated to following the Laws of the One God, we have built the Great City of the Door, and we are teaching all of the people the Truths that you taught to us. Come to us now, our Priestess, and show us a way to continue the peace."

A brilliant sliver of light pierced through a crevice in the ceiling of the temple, spreading out to surround the three people seated around the Crystal Skull. The Skull changed from its clear translucence to a rainbow of colors, first inside the object, and then shooting out to project a mass of vivid swirling forms. Gradually, the forms, melting and separating, seemed to take on a more distinct shape.

Directly above the Skull, as they watched, the shape became a woman's. The tall powerful shape of Tlacotl as they remembered her appeared to stand on air. She still wore the Quetzal feathers in her blue green headdress and cape; a turquoise mask covered her features, and the black eyes shown through the mask. Then, the mask dissolved to show Tlacotl's fine features. A feeling of such profound love and warmth emitted from the form suspended in air that the three knew she was real. Slowly standing in respect and awe, they surrounded the Priestess. Time seemed suspended until Tlacotl gently drifted from over the Skull and settled with feet on the floor. She appeared to glide rather than walk, as she took her place in the circle.

"Beloved ones," she said, "I hear your call, and as I told you those years ago, I am here watching and helping you. You have done well. You have held true to the Prophecy and to your Promise. Ask of me the questions you have. I will answer."

Morning Star said, "Oh, Mighty and Beloved Priestess, you who are able to move freely between Heaven and Earth and even into the Underworld! You who were a mother to Mockingbird and me! You who sacrificed your life here on earth to become the emissary for all that is good! We have need of your Wisdom and your Sight. We are at a crossroads and are confused about which path to take! In the midst of the Celebration of the One, which we have been building for, one comes to create disharmony. She has taken our brother in spirit, Net, the son of Turtle. We would create peace and harmony, but Mesquite is determined to create war and disharmony. How do we protect against this that our vision might be fulfilled?"

The figure of Tlacotl moved, her arms spreading the feather cloak. She emitted a golden aura, enveloping everything in the room at the top of the pyramid. Morning Star felt as if the Priestess was encompassing them in her arms, taking them with her as she viewed the situation from a higher viewpoint.

Suddenly the group who were gathered in prayer could see everything. They could see Net talking with the men at the lake, Mesquite and her son as they moved toward the city, and Jaguar running through the forest in search of his totem. They also saw themselves and their children, their friends, their neighbors, and could see all the lines of connection and disruption. Mockingbird knew she was seeing the thread of Batz, the weaver of history, and she could see all the paths that could be taken, and what the result would be if she followed each.

Now, Tlacotl lowered her arms, dropping them to her sides. She began to fade away, and Morning Star suddenly yearned for her to come back. She heard Tlacotl's voice once more:

"Daughter, I am with you. I will always come when you call."

**

An eagle circled in the sky, soaring without effort as he rode the currents of air. As Net watched, a second eagle joined the first, and a third. He had been talking to the two men from his fishing village, trying to talk them into letting him go. They had unbound his ankles, but retied his hands in front of him so he could have a little more freedom.

Cocom dropped his last fish onto a large leaf. He had quite a pile of them—plenty for their evening meal. He appeared quite pleased with his catch, but when Net asked him to release his bonds so that he might leave, Cocom's face grew taut with fear.

"We can't let you go, Net—but you won't be harmed. Mesquite captured you to have leverage in dealing with the City people."

He picked up the bundle of fish and carried them over to the fire pit. Placing them in a pot, he turned once more to Net and said, "You know I wouldn't harm you, Net. Don't worry. You will be released as soon as Mesquite gets back."

Cocom walked away into the woods. Pacal had been gathering firewood nearby as he listened to the conversation. When Cocom left, Pacal walked over near Net. He watched silently while the prisoner looked at the eagles overhead. Then he turned to see what the dozen or so men left in camp were doing.

Finally, he said, "Don't think about getting away! I'm watching you."

14

Shell decided to go out into the city and take part in the celebration. She was tired of lying about now that the pain and sickness were gone. Her auntie, Magnolia, agreed that the fresh air would be good for her.

"My daughter, there is much happening in the city. I am happy that you are well enough to go out with me," she said with gentleness.

Magnolia hadn't told Shell that Net had been taken, or that Eagle's men had gone after him. She didn't want to stress the girl and cause her to become ill again.

Magnolia helped Shell to dress for the celebration, taking great care with her clothing and hair. Shell was a beautiful girl, and Magnolia had always taken pride in her. With no children of her own, Shell had become her life. She was so happy when she learned that Net returned Shell's feelings, because she knew that Shell had always loved the young man. He was a good man, honest and true.

Some people in the village thought he was a little strange because of his communion with the sea, but Magnolia saw it as natural. Net was born in the water. His mother had been on the shore when, with one great push, she delivered her son. She hadn't even known she was in labor. The slight backache seemed natural, she said, because her belly was so large and low in the pregnancy.

At the time of Net's birth, his mother was alone. His father, Turtle, was due back from his travels, but didn't get there until the day after Net was born.

The story of Net's birth was the subject of songs and stories by all the villagers for years to come. It became a story to tell the children, of the boy who was born a fish.

Doorway Series:
Morning Star Rises

As he slid from his mother's loins, he landed in the sea.
Net's mother told how the dolphins and whales leapt from
the water, singing joyously. One dolphin, a large female,
had appeared close to the shore, and had nudged the infant
with her nose. She almost grounded herself as she pushed
the baby boy up close to his mother. When the mother
reached down and picked up her infant, the dolphin
wiggled off the sand, and returned to deeper water.

Turtle had carried the story far and wide as he went
on his trade route; and as the years passed, he brought more
tales. He told of his son, Net, whose first nursemaid had
been a dolphin; and later, of the small boy who took a ride
out into the deep sea by holding onto a dolphin's fin.

Net's mother had died several years after his birth
after she was gave birth to his stillborn sister. The tragedy
struck Turtle deeply, and he increased his time on the trade
route while the women of the village cared for Net.

Magnolia felt a deep sadness and no small amount
of guilt over Net's mother's death. Magnolia, as the
foremost midwife of the village, had been responsible for
the woman's health during her pregnancy. She couldn't
understand how the unborn infant had died—and then the
mother—when she had seemed so healthy. She was
unaware that the Shaman Ollin had foreseen that the infant
girl would become very powerful, and he had seen her as a
future threat. When he made a secret visit to Net's mother,
he gave her a medicine that killed the child. No one knew
about this, and the secret remained with Ollin.

Eventually, the grief over his wife's death destroyed
Turtle's health. He became weak and unable to eat. Net,
seeing his father waste away, turned to the sea for an
answer. His second family, the dolphins, helped him to see
the healing power of seafood. As he saw his father become
weaker, he was inspired to make a soup of seaweed. He
hoped Turtle would be able to keep it in his stomach. Long
days stretched out as Net spoon-fed his father tiny amounts

of the nourishing soup until the day came when he could eat more and more without difficulty. Gradually, he added small amounts of fish until Turtle began regaining his strength. The father and son began talking more and more; and this understanding and love was as instrumental in easing Turtle's health and grief, as was the food. Finally, the day came when the bond between father and son was whole and complete. Turtle began to see that there was something worth living for—this son of his—and he became almost like a new man. However, the long years of emotional pain had taken their toll, and Turtle never did completely recover his physical health.

He did return to his work as a Trader, walking long miles through the jungle, over the mountains, and along the seashore. Net went with him, and they both relished the time together. Now, Turtle was gone, having passed from his weakened body, but Net was happy that they had been given the opportunity to be together on that last journey.

Magnolia was certain that Turtle would be watching over his son and helping him in spirit form, so her fear for Net was eased. She also had the words of the little girl child, Feather, to bolster her courage. Feather had foretold that Net would go away, but that he would return

15

Feather was so happy! In the midst of the bustle of the city, there was so much to see and do! She had come out with Magnolia and Shell, two of her favorite people. She knew they liked being with her, too. Her earliest memories included these two as part of her family. Each woman held one of her small hands so they wouldn't lose her in the crowd.

The first thing Feather wanted to do was to watch the artisans creating their beautiful works. Potters, spinners, weavers, jewelers, basket makers and scribes all displayed their creations and worked at their arts and crafts as people watched. There were workers of soft metals, stonecutters, weapon and toolmakers, and makers of musical instruments as well.

Dancers, singers, and musicians all were on display. The singers were a special group—they were the storytellers, the poets and historians. They were philosophers. Their songs relayed to the audience their doubts and fears, their triumphs and joy. They contained the history of the people from the time of the Old Ones—the First Men—who had been their forefathers and mothers at the beginning of time. There were also the stories of the ancient gods and goddesses who had created the different worlds and ages. Everything of importance was in the poems and songs of the Singers.

The Singers were of special interest to Feather. Though she was only going on four years of age, her earliest stories included her mother's and auntie's memories of a woman they called Singer. When Mockingbird and Morning Star told her stories of Singer,

Feather could feel the love they had felt for the woman who had been their nursemaid in that temple in the other city. But even more than that, Feather knew Singer, who had died before she was born. Singer had been her guardian in spirit, and had always been visible to Feather. She had never discussed this with her mother. When she was very small, she thought everyone could see the Spirit people that she saw. Singer was with Feather even before she was born. She had helped her find her way into the womb of Mockingbird, and she had been there, talking to her, explaining things to her all of her short life. It was so natural to her that she didn't find it necessary to discuss it.

Recently, the little girl began to understand that not everyone saw Spirit people. And it was just lately that she began to see things that happened far away. So, now, she was beginning to talk to her mother and auntie about it. She felt very good about her mother telling her that she had special eyes and ears. Her mother always made her feel good about herself.

Feather began to think about Jaguar, and wished he were here so they could see all of these things together. The thought made her a little sad because she knew he didn't always want her with him.

***

Flower paced the floor in the Palace. She didn't feel up to joining the celebration with Magnolia and Shell. Her husband, Deer, had gone out with Eagle and their men, her son was in the long race, and her Queen and the Priestess were doing a private ceremony of some sort. She didn't know what caused the agitation she felt, but she couldn't sit still and rest.

She had just learned that she was carrying a child, and Morning Star had advised her to stay out of the sun for now, since she was delicate. Flower thought maybe she was worried for Deer, but his short absences from home hadn't disturbed her this much before. She didn't expect Jaguar to return to the finish line in less than two hours, so she had decided to try to nap and go out later to welcome him back. She knew that Jaguar had hoped to do well in the race, and she wanted to be there to support him no matter what happened. Sometimes she felt it was very difficult having a son who was growing up. She hoped the new baby would be a sister for Jaguar. Perhaps a daughter would be content to stay at home more than her son was. She daydreamed about all the things she could teach a daughter. She missed her own parents—especially her mother—and dreamed of recreating that same close bond with a daughter of her own.

Then she thought about the meeting with Mesquite. Of course! That must be what she was nervous about! The mere thought of the terrible looking woman with her bone necklace and her strange looks horrified her. She had really had to struggle to act as if she wasn't afraid. The meeting had almost brought back the numbing fear she had experienced as a child when her parents, against their wishes, were forced to hand her over to the Priesthood; but her determination to help her Queen and her Priestess had strengthened her ability to hold onto sanity and resolve.

16

The male jaguar opened his mouth. The sound he made, throaty and deep, was unlike any other in the jungle, and easily recognized. He was a young male, but large and supple.

His tail twitched back and forth as he smelled the air. He sniffed deeply. The air was heavy with floral scents, the musky heaviness of rotting wood, leaves and animal droppings, and pungent with the faint smell of man. A single drop of water landed on the end of his nose, falling from a large scooped leaf above him. The raucous squeal of a monkey clamored against his eardrums.

He was looking for something—he didn't know what—but, he would know it when he saw it. Looking deeply into the forest, he searched for movement. He watched the monkeys, always swinging about and raising a ruckus; but their actions were normal. They weren't warning of unusual activities. The birds, too, went about their usual business. His attention was caught momentarily with the sight of the several brightly colored hummingbirds that were hovering over a clump of flowers and feasting on nectar. He felt the need to get higher up so he could see more.

As he leapt up to a vantage point on a low branch, the large red stone, hanging from a leather thong, bounced against his white and black dappled chest. Now he heard Mother Jaguar. Bounding gracefully from the branch, he set out in the direction of her call.

The scent of humans was heavier. Female! A female had walked this path, but her scent told him she had passed some time before. Ahead lay the stronger scent of males. He continued his graceful lope.

***

The moon hung low and huge in the starry sky over the lake. As it reflected off the water, Net was filled with an ache to go for a swim. It wasn't his sea, but it was still his element. He tried to forget where he was and to think of his home where he had the freedom to do as he pleased. Now, his own people held him captive, and his heart ached for them.

Of course, it wasn't the whole village that was using him as a pawn, but there were quite a few. He understood the power that Mesquite held over them. This faction had been in existence for years. Ignited by the old Shaman, Ollin, their desire to be a part of something great was fed by the new Shaman, Mesquite. They were a simple people, but there was a thirst in them to become more than they were. First Ollin, and then Mesquite, used this need to their own advantage. Net knew all this, and wished that, somehow, they would turn their allegiance to the Enlightened Leaders who had come to fulfill the prophecy.

Net knew too, that they believed they were doing the right thing. Mesquite had told them that the Queen and the Priestess of the new City of the Door were not the true Enlightened Leaders. She told them that Ollin had known this and they killed him because of it. She told them that they were foreigners, and the prophecy had been to prepare them for someone in their own village who was the true leader.

Knowing all of this didn't make him rest any easier about his possible fate. He didn't know what they planned to do with him, and not knowing was hard to deal with. As a believer in the One, he felt he should be ready to die, but this didn't feel like the right time or place to do that. Once again, he mentally put himself with the dolphins in the sea, and this time, Shell was there with him.

Doorway Series:
Morning Star Rises

***

In the high temple on top of the tallest pyramid, the vigil was kept. All afternoon and into the night, the Priestess, the Shaman, and the Queen prayed. Flower had been asked to join them but she waited with her servers for her son to cross the finish line.

In the city, the shamans and healers from the surrounding country saw the glow of the Crystal Skull in the top of the pyramid. They didn't know what it was, but they knew it was a ceremony of highest purpose, and in their own ways and in their own nighttime shelters, they joined in with the Enlightened ones.

Others who were still about in the dark of evening saw the light, too. Gazing up at it, they wondered what was going on. Lights shot out of the temple at the top of the pyramid, casting a rainbow of color on the night sky.

17

Mesquite's doubts and mistrust of the newcomers rose to fever pitch. Turning on her band, she told them they were going back to camp. Much confusion ensued, but no one dared to confront her or to argue. Most of them were relieved, having thought about facing up to the skilled warriors of the new City, and knowing their own lack of training in this area. They turned back and arrived at the camp by dusk.

In the clearing by the lake, the first thing Mesquite looked for was her prisoner. She saw that he was awake—sitting, but bound to a tree. He seemed to have recovered from the attack. As their eyes met, Mesquite was flooded with memories of this boy as he grew up. He was one who was kind to her son, but they had never been real friends. Net was different, always a loner. His kindness to Zolin ate at her. She compared him to Zolin, and resented the ease he had in his own skin. Zolin had always been clumsy and awkward. This made her dislike Net even more.

The second thing she noticed was the rainbow of colors shooting up into the sky from the direction of the new City. The light was so bright that it dwarfed the huge moon hanging over the lake; but even the moon seemed to take on the varying hues of color. Dread stabbed into her heart at the sight. She recognized the lights as part of the usurped power of the foreigners. They had taken over the Power Place that rightfully belonged to her and her son. She knew the place the light was emanating from. When she was the Shaman's woman, he had taught her many things. One thing he taught her was that in some places the power of the Mother leaked through to join with the power of the Father—Earth and Sky coming together unhindered. The Aztec witches were not stupid. They knew that this was great power. They knew that in this place they could reach through the fog and gather together all of the strength that lay in the world of Spirit. She was very afraid.

Mesquite called her men together, but she would not show her fear to these lowly men. Standing tall and menacing, she shouted, "You are not doing your part! We are losing our power to the foreigners! Quit being so lazy and expecting me to do it all! Your lives are at risk here, not just mine, you lazy oafs! Get the fire going and prepare yourselves! We must call on Yum Cimil!"

Cowering from the High Priestess of Yum Cimil, Mesquite's men began to busy themselves. They gathered up firewood, adorned themselves with paint and the jangling necklaces of bone such as Mesquite always wore, and drank of the beverage that opened them to the spirit world. Some picked up drums and began to beat them in a slow even rhythm while the others chanted and danced.

The fire grew larger, casting shadows on the forest. All of the animals in the nearby jungle became agitated, feeling the growing force emanating from the fire and from the skeletal woman who controlled it.

From his place by the tree, Net watched. He knew they were trying to summon the god of death. He was familiar with Yum Cimil—a name he had heard in the village. It was the god of the Old Shaman, Ollin. Ollin had held secret ceremonies, not open to the whole village, but only to those whom he could intimidate. Net remembered hearing that Yum Cimil demanded blood sacrifice. He wondered nervously if Mesquite would go so far.

Eagle's troops would be at the lake in an hour. One of his soldiers had been bitten by a poisonous insect, and was feverish. He would recover, but he would only be a hindrance if they tried to carry him along. Eagle left another man behind with them. They were down two men, but the remaining five were still more skilled than Mesquite's crew. Eagle hoped that Mesquite would turn Net over without a fight. He wanted to remain true to the teachings; but he would not allow these people to intimidate them or to hurt his extended family.

***

The two cats were together now. The young male padded along beside the older female. They spoke to each other with mind pictures, and an occasional voice call that was more for emphasis than anything. The male loved his expanded senses of sight and smell. He hadn't realized how intense these could be, and how much one could know with these wonderful powers.

He could smell odors that weren't even noticed by him before, and with the scent came the knowledge of what they meant and who or what caused them. He was engulfed by the muskiness of the jungle, feeling totally free for the first time in his young life.

He padded by a large tree, split in two long ago by lightning, and knew how it had died. He smelled the deer mice in a nest under the tree, the snake coiled in rest, insects that had burrowed deep inside the wood, eating and laying eggs, and the mushrooms growing and bringing new life to the decay. The spore on the trail told him that a doe in heat had crossed here, followed shortly by a buck. His sharp eyesight caught things that he had never seen in such detail. The slightest movement registered in his awareness. The forest was alive in a way that he had never fully comprehended. He felt that he could be caught here in this body of senses, never to return to what had been before, if he wasn't careful.

18

In the palace, the nursemaid woke from the bright light dancing across her closed eyelids. She thought it was morning, and for a second, still groggy from sleep, she wondered why she hadn't awoken with the baby during the night. She looked toward the window, and was astonished to see the large moon hanging low in the sky. It appeared to have a halo of colored lights faintly surrounding it, pulsing in a regular pattern.

The room was as light as if the sun was rising and peeking in through the window. Confused, she sat up and looked over toward Star's infant to see if he was all right. What she saw caused her to catch her breath as her hand flew to her chest. The baby was lying in his cradle, wide-awake, with Feather standing beside him. Brilliant lights danced above and around them, lighting the whole room. She screamed and fainted.

***

At the camp by the lake, Mesquite felt that something was going dreadfully wrong. She searched all around, trying to discover where her discomfort was coming from. Net was still bound to the tree, so it couldn't be that. Quiet, not uttering a sound, he appeared to be sleeping as he sat there. The glow in the sky lit him from the side, causing him to look as if he was on fire.

She turned back to the fire, but doubt nagged at her, keeping her from slipping into the crevice she had created between the earth and the void. It was the place where she was able to conjure up the terrible and mighty Yum Cimil. She felt as though a barrier was thrown up, and she didn't know how to pierce it. Panic seized her, blocking her passage even more. She tried to get hold of her power, but it felt as though it slipped between her fingers. The more she grasped at it, the more it evaded her.

***

Shell awoke with a start. Magnolia lay next to her, snoring softly. From their room in the palace, Shell could see a strange glow outside. She rose gently, trying not to disturb her Auntie, and tiptoed to the window.

The plaza was empty but for a small group of shamans and healers, gathered in a circle at the foot of the Temple of Quetzalcoatl. The night sky was awash with lights, a rainbow of colors extending as far as the eye could see. From the group on the plaza, up to the top of the temple, and beyond into the heavens, pulsing lights of every hue highlighted everything in a glow so beautiful it took Shell's breath away. Reflecting from the heavens and back onto the plaza, the light bathed the City in a magical glow. Earth reached out to Sky as they joined energies. The water in the fountains was alive with light, the stone and earth glowed, and the flowers, grasses, and trees radiated their own beauty. The small group of people in the plaza emitted such beautiful light and colors that Shell was overwhelmed. Everything in the city was aglow. The light holders in the plaza gave their energy to the light movers in the top of the temple, all working together with the One God of Duality to change destiny.

***

In her sleep, Magnolia joined her energies with those of the light workers. With good heart, but not quite as advanced as the others, she still made a difference.

Net, under the tree in the camp by the lake, reached out, too. He called to the dolphins in the sea, his second family, to hold the light from there. They, in turn, gave the signal to the whales.

The soldiers in the forest, on their way to the camp of Mesquite, felt the pull and saw the light. They stopped where they were and prayed to be as one with the others. Then, from a distance, they heard Jaguar roar. It was a call that couldn't be denied, and they moved on, still holding the energy.

Not since the First Men had there been such a unity of spirit, with humans, animals, plant life, and the very Earth working together as one, in the ways of Light.

19

Jaguar roared, a deep rumble in his throat—a sound
that made a shiver run up Net's spine and caused the hair to
stand up on the back of his neck. It wasn't fear that caused
this reaction in his body, but hope. Net recognized the
sound of Jaguar as a promise and he opened his eyes. He
saw the confusion and indecision in the group of
worshippers at the fire, as they stared at the sky. A comet
shot through the air, exploding in a shower of sparks as
they watched. Burning embers dropped from the sky,
landing all around. They ran from their places, seeking
protection under the trees and leaving Mesquite by herself
with the fire.

She turned, anger shooting from her close-set eyes,
and stomped toward Net, purposeful in her rage. As she
moved toward him, she heard a groaning and rumbling of
the earth as the ground heaved beneath her feet. Falling to
the ground, she looked frantically around to see what had
caused this. She heard the rumble again as the earth split in
front of her. Between the maddened priestess of Yum Cimil
and the bound prisoner, a huge chasm appeared. She lay
there, holding to the ground, trying to find something solid
to hang onto while the comet's burning clumps fell all
around her. She looked to the forest and saw her son, Zolin,
unable to move as he clung to a tree. Rage replaced by
panic, Mesquite was helpless, a pawn of the elements and
the greater power of the Light Movers.

As she lay on the ground and stared into Net's eyes
as if to ask why and how, she saw two jaguars pad up
slowly behind him. Fire still rained from the sky, narrowly
missing Mesquite, and threatening to start the forest ablaze.

She didn't even notice as she watched, mesmerized, to see what was happening across the chasm at the tree that held Net hostage. He looked back at her, feeling utterly at peace, as he waited calmly to see what would happen next.

The low rumble of the young male jaguar seemed to come from right behind Net. Allowing his head to turn toward the sound, he saw two jaguars. Still in a dream state, he watched without reaction as the jaguars moved toward him. Then, the larger female held back, waiting as the young male padded slowly toward Net. He saw the beautiful body of the cat, golden with black rosettes, green eyes ablaze, mouth open as if to speak. It moved with such grace that it seemed unreal.

Net's gaze was caught by the large red stone as it moved gently against the tawny breast of the large cat. Net knew that stone, that necklace made of thong and ruby fire. Its glow became brighter, competing with the greens of the forest light and the shooting colors of the sky. As Net watched, the jaguar gradually changed form. Rising from his hands and knees, the boy, Jaguar, stood. His young body seemed to still carry remnants of the grace of the cat, but it was the boy who moved toward Net and loosed his bonds.

**

In the high temple, overlooking the treetops surrounding the city, the Priestess spoke: "It is done."

Morning Star, Priestess of the One, follower of the Great Quetzalcoatl, spoke quietly but with finality. She still sat in the circle, looking into the Crystal Skull. In it, she saw the events that had taken place at Mesquite's camp by the lake. She saw that no lives had been forfeited and that the Light had won out. She saw that her loved ones and her people were safe.

Her comrades, still in altered consciousness, slowly opened their eyes and waited for the Priestess to say more. Before them, they saw a young woman with a soul as ancient as the First Men—no, even older. This woman they had known since childhood had reached into her soul memories and had known what to do. She knew how to create, using the gift of the One. She knew that the power of Light, held by enough people, could overcome any darkness.

As Mockingbird looked to Morning Star, it seemed that she was almost translucent; and beyond her, she could see other figures. As if lined up in a row, one behind the other, and each succeeding figure a little higher than the previous, were men, women and children. Mockingbird realized that these other figures were representative of Morning Star's past-life selves, somehow all coming together to work with her present-day self in order to add strength to her work. Mockingbird didn't know how she knew this—she just did.

Having just come out of a night long vigil of deepest meditation, this knowledge didn't seem strange or out of the ordinary. She slowly looked around at the others in the circle, and saw the same manifestation with each of them. She knew that she must look the same to the others.

Slowly and gently, each of them started to move, blinking their eyes and stretching. As each came back in greater connection with their physical bodies, the ghostly past-life forms seemed to fade, leaving only a vague imprint in the minds of the participants.

Once again, the Priestess said, "It is done."

***

The baby's nurse opened her eyes. Sunlight was streaming in the window. She remembered vaguely some sort of a dream she had the previous night about the infant, Light, and the girl, Feather. She couldn't bring the memory back; she only knew it had been a frightening dream to her.

She rolled over and saw Feather asleep beside her. She wondered when the child had come in to sleep with her. Then she remembered a fragment of the dream she had the night before. A hazy picture washed through her mind of the girl standing beside the cradle. Then it came flooding back, and her heart pounded within her chest as she became sure that the events had actually happened.

Ayah, I am lucky! I am blessed to be able to care for these great ones. Ayah, ayah!

20

Once again the plaza was filled with people from far and wide. A renewed feeling of expectation filled the air. No one had gone untouched during the vigil. Each and every one in the city and surrounding area had been a part of the larger soul group, each contributing in their own way, whether awake or asleep. Their lives would never be the same. A sense of purpose had come of the unity, and a bond that would forever tie them together. Some were consciously aware of this, while others knew it only at soul level.

Even those who weren't consciously aware felt it; they felt as if they were waiting for something. Every one of them was there in that place and at that time for a reason. They had agreed to work together for peace before they had even come into the earth this lifetime.

Morning Star held out her hands, palm up. The golden flecks seemed to pass right through her body, and disappear into the temple beneath her feet.

As quickly as this manifestation appeared, it disappeared, as the sun rose in its usual course. The ceremony had ended, but everyone seemed frozen in place. After a moment, they all looked around and at each other for confirmation that they had all experienced the same thing.

At the line between the city and the forest, a group of weary travelers appeared. They weren't at first observed by anyone, as all were grouped in front of the temple.

Even though it was a huge gathering of people, the city was much larger. It had been built in the distant past by a group of travelers from distant regions. When their seers foretold the destruction of Aztlan, they came to this place to make a new home. They had advanced knowledge of the land where this city was built. They knew it was a place of high energy where the breath of Earth joined with the breath of Sky. As they settled here, the native tribes came to see what they were about, and many joined them in the construction of the city.

The travelers from Aztlan had much knowledge and they shared it generously with the natives of the land. Singers still carried these stories from place to place, relating the history of the People. The songs were a thread that held all the people of the land together. They all had a common history and all had similar songs of heroes and heroines, of gods and goddesses, and of the ages of man.

All of these varying sea people and mountain people and forest people knew the songs. They knew how the earth was formed, and the heavens. They knew that Earth was a living form, and that She breathed spirit in and out. When they stood at the mouth of her caves, they could hear her breath. They knew that the Earth had been created four times before, and destroyed. They lived in the beginning of the fifth world. They knew, too, when this one would end.

They understood the planets and stars, knowing that they, too, were living forms. They understood that the sky walkers moved in certain paths, and that they had a relationship to what happened on Earth.

The people understood, too, that all things were living beings, and had a place and purpose. They knew that all of it—the Earth, the Sky, the creatures and people—were all parts of the One Great God in Two Forms, the Lord of Duality.

***

A solitary form was also entering the city from a different path. This person didn't see the golden flecks falling from above. He didn't feel the joy that the others

felt. He was intent on something else, and his vibrations
weren't at the right level to be able to discern the miracle.
His lanky ungainly frame slid from tree to bush and from
monument to fountain, keeping out of sight as much as
possible. He knew where he wanted to go, so he entered the
city as close to his objective as possible.

21

The meetings of the Wise Ones—the civic and spiritual leaders from all the different places that had met in the temples of the city—were postponed until the following day. Instead, a meeting was held between the returning soldiers and the ones who had stayed in the city. Eagle, Deer, Net and Jaguar met with Morning Star, Mockingbird, Snake and Flower.

There was much to tell. Net started out by telling the group about his abduction. He told them of how he woke with a sore head and found himself belly down on the earth, tied with his hands behind him, and his feet tied to his hands. He said he had been taken with shock and sadness when he saw men from his own village, acting as though it was normal to do this to a childhood friend. He continued his story, telling every detail. Finally, he told them about Mesquite coming back, very angry about something, and how she shouted at her people to build a fire for a ceremony. His blood ran cold as he acted out the part of Mesquite, saying, "Blood he shall have!" He confided that he wondered if she was planning on shedding his blood—and, as he sat helplessly tied to the tree, he was unable to defend himself or to run. But, he said, as he watched the lights in the sky and heard jaguar roar, he knew that everything would be all right.

Then Eagle and Deer took turns telling about their journey. They told how a poisonous insect struck one of their men, and he had to be left behind on the trail with another to care for him. They told how they kept hearing jaguar call out to them, and knew they were being watched over. They talked about the amazing colored lights in the sky—the beauty of the vigil shining forth.

With great theatrics, they told of the groaning of the earth, the shaking of the ground beneath their feet, and of how Mesquite's men practically threw themselves at the feet of the soldiers. They described the violent thrust of the Earth as She split apart, and the firestorm of burning rocks that rained from the Sky.

Again, Net continued the story, telling of how the Earth created a giant chasm between him and Mesquite, just as she was headed toward him with hatred in her eyes—and of the jaguar who walked up behind him—the giant cat with the ruby necklace who turned into his young friend, Jaguar, right before his eyes!

"I tell you!" Deer confirmed the story. "My son is a shape shifter! He is a holy one, as we have known since his infancy!"

Deer smiled with wonder at his son and then at his wife. Flower, in shock with this revelation, clutched her heart with her graceful slender hand.

"My son, is this true? Surely your father jokes?"

"It is true, Nantli."

"How can you do this, Son?"

Jaguar looked thoughtful as he scratched his head. "I just see the jaguar in my head, Nantli. Then the stone I wear grows warm, and soon I am looking through jaguar's eyes and feeling with his body. I smell with his nose, and I look down to see his feet in place of my own."

Flower beheld her son with awe. He looked like any eight-year-old boy, but he was Shaman! Thinking of the danger he had been in, Flower feared for her son. But she knew he had been under the protection of the One, and she knew it was his destiny.

Jaguar said, "Nantli, I am tired and hungry. May I go rest?"

Flower looked to Morning Star for affirmation.

Morning Star said, "Jaguar, you have done well. We will talk later. Go now to eat and rest."

The boy, barely able to keep his eyes open, left the group of elders and went to his quarters with a server. He felt happy that his family approved of what he had done. It had come so naturally to him that he wasn't sure why they seemed to think it was worth praising him. Now, all he could think of was something to fill his empty stomach, and a cushion to lie on.

Once Jaguar had left, Snake said, "He is still in training at the Calmecac. We will make sure that he continues to be trained in the right way."

Mockingbird asked, "My husband, where are your men?"

"They all are back in the City, My Queen. The one who was injured is in the Temple of Healing where he is being cared for. The others are resting up to be ready for the Ceremonies today."

She nodded. "And the men of Mesquite?"

"We told them to go home, My Queen. They were shaken badly with the events."

"And Mesquite, Zolin, and Wolf?"

"We did not see Wolf or Zolin. Mesquite disappeared as we were rounding up her men. She was lying on the ground when we got there; but when I looked again, she was gone. We searched the forest, but we could not find her."

Mockingbird breathed a deep sigh. She wasn't sure what they would have done with Mesquite if she had been brought back, so this was probably the best thing. She said, "We have a Ceremony to attend. Let us celebrate!"

***

The women, responsible for creating and leading a new nation, were dedicated mothers. As they made their way through the palace to the nursery, they talked about their children.

Doorway Series:
Morning Star Rises

Morning Star said, "Flower, you are truly blessed to have such a son as Jaguar. He has a great destiny awaiting him. He is a holy child, and you are responsible for having helped to guide him in the ways of the One."

Flower answered, "Priestess, I thank you. I know he is blessed, but I also know he will have challenges, and he must be taught to always follow the ways. I must admit I am often frightened for him, though I know he is guided. I feel ashamed to admit this fear."

Morning Star thought about what Flower had said. Then she answered, "Sister, you have nothing to feel shame about. It is because you are a loving mother that you want your son to be safe. It is the way mothers are created, because children need to be cared for and watched over. You know the dangers that await your son and you love him deeply. Still, you do not keep him from fulfilling his destiny, even though it would be easier for you. This is as it should be."

As they entered the nursery, little Feather was on the floor, playing with Light. The baby was crawling now, and when the women entered, he looked up and laughed. Feather ran to her mother for a hug.

Light pushed himself into sitting position, and gurgled as he slapped his hands on the beam of sunlight coursing through the window to dance upon the floor. The women looked on fondly, and laughed gently at his play.

Papan, the nursemaid, stood twisting a cloth in her hands, and looked as though she needed to say something.

Mockingbird said, "Papan, what it is? You look as though you are about to burst from holding your words!"

"My Queen...Priestess... Lady..."

Papan was unable to continue. She looked at the floor.

"Come, Papan, you have no need to fear. Speak!"

"Very well, My Queen. It is just that...just that...oh, I am unsure how to tell you this..."

Feather spoke up. "Nantli, Papan is trying to tell you what happened last night."

Mockingbird chastised Feather, "Daughter, let Papan speak for herself."

"Forgive my rudeness, Papan."

Papan smiled gently at Feather. "You are forgiven, child."

Then, looking at Mockingbird she said, "Forgive me, my Queen, for stumbling over my words. I will tell you as it happened. Sometime during the night, I awoke to a great light in the room. It was so bright, I thought I had overslept. But then, I looked to see if the little one was still sleeping, and what I saw caused my soul to take flight. It left my body and did not come back until the sun rose!"

The Queen prodded her gently, "And what was it that caused you such fright, Papan?"

"It was...I saw...the children..." Papan began to weep.

Mockingbird's heart went out to the distraught nursemaid, and she put an arm around her shoulders, calming her with her will. Finally, Papan was able to speak.

"It was the children, my Queen. The infant was awake and Feather stood beside his cradle. A halo of colored lights surrounded them, coming from them, it seemed—as if they were torches, and at first I thought they were on fire! I was so frightened! Then I saw that the lights were not fire, but beauty beyond belief—the children glowed like the moon and the stars! It was too much for me, my Queen, and I fell back on my bed in a faint. I knew nothing more until I awoke this morning. I am sorry, my Ladies. I should have made sure the children were safe. I am but a weak woman who should not be caring for children!" Papan broke down with weeping once again.

Morning Star comforted her. "Papan, do not weep so! You are the best of nurses to our children. They are blessed to have your soft body to comfort them and your gentle heart to guide them. You are like the nurse I had as a child—my beloved Singer. This is why I asked you to care for my son! I have never forgotten Singer, who is always in my heart—and I know these children here will always love you, Papan! You give everything to their care!"

Feather ran to Papan, and put her little arms about her nurse.

"Papan," she said, "we do love you. My little brother tells me many things. He does not want you to cry!"

Papan smiled through her tears and said, "Child, how does this babe speak to you?"

"I can hear his thoughts, my Nurse. When you thought we were on fire, it was the light that we were moving. My brother told me we needed to move the light."

Morning Star looked upon the children with joy. She said, "Sisters, we are blessed beyond all in our children. What wonder and glory we have been allowed by the Great One that he would allow these souls to come from our loins, and be given to us for guidance!"

22

In the tunnels beneath the palace, the lone figure searched. He had been here when he closed the door on the Queen. He had a long memory, and he hated her with all of his being.

He remembered as he searched for the openings to the tunnels. He remembered what she had done, and his anger grew.

For his entire life, he had been successful in keeping the abandoned city from intrusion by anyone. When he had discovered it, he recognized the great power of the land on which it was built. He knew this was to be his capitol—the place of power from which he would rule the world. He frightened the people, telling them that it was a city of death; and if they entered it, they would surely die. He was waiting, building his following, and planning for the day when he would make his grand entrance into the city and all would fall at his feet.

Then, the day came when the small band of Aztecs entered his village. When he saw his people's reaction, he was filled with horror. They believed that these ragged travelers were the Enlightened Rulers of Prophecy! He was frightened as his hopes and plans seemed to turn to dust before his eyes. He could not—would not—allow this to happen! The problem was, he didn't have time to plan—time to devise a way to stop them.

His people adored the newcomers with a dedication and passion that should have been reserved for him. Quickly, he used his wits. He would have a ceremony of welcome in his calli—with only these present—and he would poison the one he saw was the leader. Just as she—the new queen—was about to drink of the poison he gave her, the seer knocked the cup from her hands. It was as if she knew what he had planned. He bluffed his way through it, pretending righteous indignation that they would dare to defile his ceremony in this way. He didn't need to feign the anger that smoldered inside him.

Then came the time for the Aztecs to leave. He knew they planned to take over his city in the forest. He gathered some of his men and went to stop them. Yet again, he hadn't had time to plan it all out. So, he tried merely to kill the one who would be queen. She must have had great magic, because the arrow struck another, and his prey escaped. The Aztec soldiers, along with the traitors from his village, dispersed his followers. He escaped to a raft he had hidden by the river, and he thought he had gotten away when a barrage of arrows flew at him. He managed to avoid the arrows, and jumped into the river amidst a number of hungry crocodiles. With his sharp knife, he slashed one of them, and as the others flew into blood frenzy, he had escaped to the shore. He hid in the reeds until the Aztecs quit searching for him.

That had been almost four years before. During that time, he hid away in a cave—knowing the superstition of the people would preserve his secret. They were frightened of the doors to the underworld—but not he! Not Ollin!

***

Ollin happened to be near the lake where Net was imprisoned and he saw Mesquite as she performed her ritual to the god of death. He saw that her men did not respect her, and how lazy they were. He witnessed the comet as it exploded in the sky, dropping a rain of fire on Mesquite's group.

"Ah, she has lost her power!" He was amazed at the violence of the Earth as it tried to shake Mesquite from its surface. He saw the split in the ground, the split that had stopped Mesquite from dragging Net to the sacrificial altar.

Doorway Series:
Morning Star Rises

Ollin had seen how displeased the gods were with Mesquite. When the soldiers were busy with her men, he caught her attention and motioned for her to come to him. She had taken drink before the ceremony, the drug that helped her to connect with the god of death. So, when she saw Ollin motioning to her, she thought she had opened the veil to the other side, and she came to him as to a god. She hadn't been aware that Ollin lived. No one knew, not even this woman who had been so enraptured with him. She flew to him, believing his spirit would save her from this devastation.

She gazed upon his face, saying, "Ah...you have come for me from the Underworld! You have come to save me!"

He had forgotten how ungainly the woman was...or perhaps, it was because she had been younger when he had taken her as his lover. Her youth and enthusiasm had made up for her lack of beauty, but she was no longer young. She had always been greedy and power-hungry. He knew that it was his power that had attracted her. He wasn't foolish enough to believe it was his fine features or his muscular body—he knew he had never been attractive to women.

Now, he was looking for reasons to do what he had to do. He motioned to Mesquite, playing the game that he was a spirit, come back for her. After walking for a long time, she was beginning to wear down.

"Shaman!" She cried out to him. "Shaman! You have come for me from the Underworld?"

"Yes," he said. "I come from the Underworld for you, Mesquite!"

She thrilled at the thought. Surely he must have loved her after all!

Finally, they neared the cave where he had been living for all this time. He had stayed there, sleeping in the mouth of the underworld, going out only to hunt game and to spy on the city. No one knew he still lived, and it gave him time to plan. He would not go against the Aztecs again without a plan! He had stayed near the mouth of the cave, except for when he wanted to worship the gods. Then, he ventured deeper inside, but always—always with a sacrifice. He did not dare to anger his gods.

***

Snake let his spirit fly as he looked for Mesquite. As he thought about her, he instantly found himself hovering near her. She was lying on a rock ledge in what appeared to be a cave. Down below the ledge, water flowed in an underground river. It was a long drop to the river from where she was. He wondered how she had gotten there. He didn't see anyone else around.

Mesquite was bruised and dirty with burn spots marring her arms and legs. Her clothing was torn and burned. The necklace of bone that was always around her neck was no longer there. She appeared to be awake, but when she struggled to sit up, she fell back. Then, Snake saw that her hands and feet were bound.

Next to where she lay, he saw what appeared to be the ashes of many old fires, one laid upon the other, the cold grey ashes mingled with animal bones. Above the fire pit, the walls were covered with paintings. Snake could see that this was a ceremonial site. He thought it must have been pretty deep into the cave, but he didn't know which cave it was. It didn't look familiar to him, though he had been in several caves near the city. These were holy places, paths to the Underworld. Some were inhabited by souls of the deceased, it was said; but he didn't see any.

"My Wife," he said, "we don't need to concern ourselves with the idea that Mesquite may be trying some new form of attack. She is not in a position to harm anyone. Instead, it is she who seems to be in trouble."

23

As Ollin entered the underground tunnel leading into the bowels of the Earth under the Palace, he had a realization—he knew that he had almost made a terrible mistake. His gods would not be pleased with his gift of Mesquite. He didn't know how he could have been so blind. They would be angry about the poor offering. What he needed was a young and beautiful virgin if he hoped to satisfy them! He would have to think on this.

He had been in the tunnel before—when the pretender to the throne had been there. He recalled how he had followed her from a distance, watching and waiting for his chance. Finally, he decided the easiest way to get rid of her was to lock her in the tunnels and let her starve to death—a slow painful death—and one which couldn't be traced back to him. It was what she deserved, he told himself, for taking what rightfully belonged to others. She was an Aztec, and this wasn't Aztec land! Besides that, she was a woman!

Somehow, though, she had been freed. When he learned this, he had been furious. What kind of power did this usurper have? He railed against his gods for letting this happen. He knew that she and her priestess were said to worship only one god, but he couldn't see how this could be. It had to be some perverted idea they brought with them from the foreign land.

He hadn't talked with anyone for over the three years that he had been waiting and planning. He had seen people from hiding, but he hadn't come in direct contact with anyone. This solitude had hardened his hatred for the two women, and his fantasies about how he would get even were constantly on his mind.

The biggest problem that he foresaw was that the women had become increasingly popular with the local inhabitants. He needed a way to turn the people against them. He searched his mind, trying out different scenarios.

Finally, he came up with a plan. In his excursions into the city before the foreigners arrived, he had searched for the lost treasury of the ancient people who had once lived there. He had been in these tunnels long before the time when he had locked Mockingbird in, and he had found the treasury. It had been much grander than his greedy dreams had even suggested. He was certain that he could use the great wealth to purchase power.

His route from outside the palace walls was secreted in a place they wouldn't have been able to find unless they were searching for it. He only knew of it because he had been in the tunnels by way of the interior and had accidentally found this way out. The opening was so well hidden that even he wouldn't have found it by searching from the outside.

He decided the best way to undermine the new leaders was through wealth. With enough wealth, he could buy the loyalty of many. He was certain he could take more of the jewels and golden ornaments out of the treasury and begin laying them up for the future. This large gathering of people was perfect for his plan. The leaders would be distracted by all of their ceremonies and they wouldn't notice one more person in the city.

He knew his looks had changed a lot in the last few years. He had become lean with the need to fend for himself. He was scarred from battles with his prey and battered from the elements. On top of all this, his hair had turned gray and he was now covered with tattoos he had self-inflicted. His clothing was made of animal skins and bird hides. He was sure that no one who had known him in the past would recognize him now.

He had developed his plan further than this, but for the present, he would get out as much gold and gems from the treasury as he could. It would be a good start, and once he gained control of the city, he would have free access to all of it—the whole treasury and all of the power it represented.

***

Jaguar requested a meal from the palace server as he headed for the bath. His muscles ached from all he had been through, and the thought of the warm spring waters put speed into his step. He bypassed the steam bath and allowed a servant to scrub him down with xixi, a soap made from vegetables, and to rinse him. Then he plunged into the flower-scented bath, diving under the water to emerge with a shake of his thick black hair. Jaguar turned on his back to float, allowing his muscles to relax. Finally, he turned over and swam back to the edge of the bath, as Net had taught him. The motion of swimming further loosened his muscles. Finally, he climbed out on the side of the pool rather than to walk up the stairs. He pulled himself out of the water, his youth allowing him to bounce back from the strain. After the servant dried him and gave him clean clothing, Jaguar hurried back to his quarters to eat.

When he arrived, he found Feather waiting for him. Her back toward him, she was arranging food on a table. She must have decided to eat with him, as the table was set for two. He stood quietly, listening to her pretty voice, as she sang a song of gratitude to the One. Then she stood back to survey her work. He had to smile at the grace of the serious little girl as she finished her preparations.

As if she knew he was behind her, Feather turned to Jaguar. "Please sit, Brother, and eat," she said.

He answered, "You surprised me, Younger Sister! Does Papan know you are here?"

Doorway Series:
Morning Star Rises

"Yes, Brother. You needn't worry. Papan tells me that I am a very big girl now but that I must always tell her where I am going. She said that the people who took me before might try to do it again, so I should only leave my room with a server or a family member. Cuixtli brought me here. Wasn't he standing outside the door when you came in?"

"Yes he was, Sister, and I told him he should not stand so long on that bad leg. He is getting very old."

"He is old, Brother, but he wants to serve the Queen's family."

Jaguar was embarrassed to be chastised by his little friend. He changed the subject. "Did Papan not feed you, Sister?"

"Oh, she would have, but I told her that I wished to eat with you. I hoped you would tell me all about your adventure!"

"I am weary, Feather," he said. "Can we not talk about this tomorrow?"

Disappointed, Feather said, "Very well, but may I eat with you?"

He motioned for the small girl to be seated. He asked, "And what have we?"

Feather, blue eyes sparkling in her animated face, said, "Many wonderful foods, my Brother! Papan sent a server to the plaza to buy from the vendors. We have foods from the sea and the mountains and the plains and the forest!"

"See!" She pointed to the various treats as she spoke. "We have dried fish, and soup, and corn cakes sweetened with honey, and this is turkey with peppers and tomatoes!"

The table was laden with exotic dishes, making Jaguar's mouth water.

There were many dishes Jaguar had never seen before, and he was so hungry that he took some food from each dish. They both ate with gusto, Feather barely pausing between bites to daintily wipe her mouth.

***

Snake led Eagle and Deer through the forest, looking for the signs he had noticed when he had been out-of-body.

While watching Mesquite in the cave, he had been visited by a being of great light who told him that she could be saved from her crooked path if he would rescue her. He didn't have any doubts when this Light Being came to him. It was the one he has seen when he had almost died from the bite of the jumping snake, which had sent him to the other world.

Snake had learned many wonders from this Being. Greatest of all, he was shown who he really was. Up to that point in his life, he thought he knew who he was. His experiences had taught him that he was a former citizen of Tula, a follower of the Great Quetzalcoatl who had been a mighty messenger from the One. This Quetzalcoatl had taught the simple message that All is One. He had thought he understood it, and he did on a basic level. He knew he had been captured by the Aztec army and then became a household slave to a soldier. He saw himself as being a pawn of fate or the decree of the One God. He didn't really see the part he played in creating his own destiny.

When the jumping snake had bitten him, the Light Being came to him. It showed Snake his real self. It showed him that he was a great Shaman, and just hadn't recognized it yet. It showed him that he had the ability to do great things—things he had dreamed of, but didn't believe were possible.

He thought about these things as he pushed his way through the jungle. The path to the cave wasn't well used. It was overgrown and very few knew of its location. He realized that someone knew, but he wasn't sure who it was who had been living there or who bound Mesquite far back in the caverns. He has seen that it was a place used in the old days, and that animal sacrifices had been made there. He could read most of the writing on the walls of the cavern, and what he read had explained some questions he had. It was the horrible story of the downfall of a great civilization.

A shiver ran up his spine as he thought of these things. Since being told of his Shamanic abilities, Snake believed it was possible. He studied with the Old Priestess who had died by the arrow that Ollin had meant for the Queen.

After that, Snake studied with the New Priestess, Morning Star, who later became his wife. His life became so much more than he ever expected. When he had lived in darkness, he happily accepted his lot, but since opening up to the Light, he had found true joy. Morning Star had given him a beautiful son who already, in infancy, showed signs of greatness. He felt so blessed and was so grateful to the One God he served.

His mind, ever on the move, once more settled on the woman, Mesquite. The Light Being had told him that she was not completely lost. It told him that her heart could be opened to love of others and to the One, so he knew it was true. He knew that all people had the ability to choose good, no matter how hidden the light or how distorted the mind might be. This thought renewed his energy, and his step quickened.

Cutting through a tough vine, he said to his companions, "This way, Soldiers! We are close now. I remember seeing the mountain from this view, and there are the three old trees that look as though they started as one. They are very unique. See how it looks like that one is pointing? It looks like an arm with a hand if you look just right. It points toward the cavern where Mesquite is!"

Eagle said, "Honored Shaman, that is very handy magic you have—the ability to send your spirit from your body!"

Deer said, "Indeed, Shaman! Can you teach it to Deer and me? It would save us many miles and worn sandals!"

Snake laughed, "I can try, Soldiers! You must keep a pure heart and a desire to be one with all. I am not sure that the desire to save on sandals is enough, though."

Deer said, "I am glad you still have a sense of humor, Snake. You have always had a way of lightening the darkest of times!"

Just as he said this, they came to a small clearing, and Snake walked toward a clump of foliage.

"It is here," he said. "Just behind these bushes!"

24

Morning Star stood in front of the group of shamans, seers, priests and priestesses in the Temple of Healing. Wearing a simple white shift, a brilliant multi-colored woven belt, and the red sandals that Flower had made for her, she was a vision of grace and loveliness. Her thick blue-black hair was dressed in the simple style she had gotten used to on the long journey to the new city from the Aztec capitol. On the trail with no slaves along to do the intricate hairstyles, she and the other women started wearing their hair down, tied back or in long braids to keep it out of their eyes. The small scar on Morning Star's forehead was covered with a polished blue jade, attached with a headband of silver. This piece was one that Mockingbird had recovered from the underground treasury before it filled with water, and had given to Morning Star.

As the Priestess spoke to the assemblage about her life, the blue jade seemed to sparkle at times, throwing out streams of light from deep within the stone. An excellent storyteller, her body and movements told as much as her words. The audience was enthralled. As she looked at them, she was filled with gratitude. Thirty of the most dedicated people in the land were assembled in this room. She had gotten to know them all during these teaching/learning times during the Oneness Festival.

Every day was one of sharing their own histories and perspectives, while at the same time, being at the Celebration to learn what they could. In each village, the people had, as part of their history, the prophecy—the prophecy of the Enlightened Leaders! They were hungry for the knowledge that Morning Star imparted to them about the mysteries. They were eager for the discussions surrounding the Laws of the One. It was a joyous and uniting time.

What they learned from Morning Star was the truth that all are one—that they were all a part of the whole, and that they were here to learn and take all they had learned back to the One. They learned that when they hurt others, they were hurting themselves; and that when they loved one another, they loved themselves. The Great Prophet, Quetzalcoatl, taught all of these things to the ancient peoples. He had taught these truths to the Grandfathers and Grandmothers, but over time, many of the teachings were lost or perverted.

Morning Star especially loved their discussions about astronomy and astrology. They all knew that the stars and planets were living beings, just as Grandmother Earth was alive and conscious of the Laws. They discussed how everything moved in cycles, and how there was no beginning and no end. They knew that change was constant, and that every being, be it rock or tree or person, was always changing and evolving.

"Honored Priestess!" The Shaman, Tototl, from the mountain area, requested permission to speak. He was a small man, strong in the legs, and dressed in woven clothing of brilliant reds, blues, and greens. His short graying hair touched the bottoms of his large ears, and his warm compassionate eyes crinkled at the corners as he smiled at Morning Star.

"Speak, Shaman!" Morning Star couldn't help but smile back.

"Honored Priestess, it is rumored that you are the Holder of the Great Crystal Skull!" The statement was really a question, but propriety and custom did not allow the Shaman to pose it directly.

"This is true, Shaman..." Morning Star paused, her small smile replaced with a frown of concentration. As if reaching a decision, she visibly straightened and walked closer to the group. She sat with them, ready to share this marvelous gift with them.

"Honored Friends," she began. "I have been planning to discuss this with you in time, but since Shaman Tototl has asked, this is the proper time. My old teacher, the blessed Priestess who was as a mother to me, and who taught me her secret knowledge, gave the Great Crystal Skull to me. I say she gave it to me, but it was not as a possession. It was passed into my hands to be its guardian and because I was compatible with it."

Morning Star's emotions were too strong for her to sit with her companions. She rose, speaking softly, but with intensity, as she moved toward the altar. "When my Teacher saw that the Great Skull glowed and vibrated in answer to my touch, she knew that I was the next in line to be the Holder. She told me that it would only respond to its true Holder, and that if someone not initiated in the Laws of the One tries to use it, the Crystal Skull would remain as if dead."

The listeners did not ask questions—it would have been rude to break in on the Great Priestess as she told her story—but they all leaned forward, listening eagerly to the soft voice.

Morning Star continued, "My Beloved Friends, the Old Priestess taught me many things, but the Great Crystal Skull seemed to know me even before I felt I was ready for the responsibility. One thing she did tell me, though—and this is very important! She taught me that the Great Skull is not a god. It was formed from a giant crystal formation by the First Men. You all, as men and women who communicate with the One, know that crystal has many wonderful properties. It is a living rock, capable of growing and reproducing. It is able to hold energies and to magnify the output of energies."

Her eyes flashed as she told them the stories she had heard from the Priestess Tlacotl, when she had been a student.

"The First Men were wise and knew many of the secrets of the One. They had strong magic, and were able to do things that seem impossible. They could talk to each other from many miles distance. They had boats that were able to go under the water as well as on top. They also had boats that flew through the air. Many, many mysteries were common to them. They knew how to use the Power of the Crystal. But the most amazing magic is here in this room with us."

The room was hushed as Morning Star moved to the altar and pulled back the golden cloth, revealing the Great Crystal Skull.

Behind her, Morning Star heard the intake of breath and felt the anticipation. She turned to her fellow seers and said, "Please join me in activating this gift. Perhaps you have questions that can be answered by it. It is the repository of knowledge from before time!"

She turned to the others and began a slow chant, moving her dancer body in rhythm as she chanted. One by one, the others joined in. The perfectly pitched chant grew strong and clear in the air and the Great Crystal Skull began to vibrate, emitting a soft greenish glow that seemed to grow until it filled the room.

***

Deep beneath the Palace, Ollin followed the trail he had taken when he had locked Mockingbird into the tunnels. He knew that somehow she had been released, and it angered him, but he was not about to let it stop him from his plans. This would be his last trip until the Queen was deposed and he had control of the City.

There were several highly prized pieces of jade—small statuettes and jewelry—that would be easy to carry, and that were worth a fortune. He felt driven to see the treasury again, to fortify his resolve, and to grab these last pieces before settling down once again to wait. He told himself, *It won't be long, now.*

Feeling renewed, he reached the door he had closed on the Queen. He easily found the trigger to open it, and for the first time in years, he smiled. As he released the mechanism to the door that had been sealed tight since Mockingbird escaped, the pent up water pushed out with such force, it knocked him from his feet. Rammed against the wall of the tunnel, the breath knocked from his lungs, his head smashed against the stone. It was so sudden that the smile remained. He looked almost peaceful in his watery grave.

***

Snake, Deer and Eagle cautiously sidestepped along the high ledge over the underground river. Stalactites hung from the ceiling and were attached to the sides of the cavern in areas, making it hard for them to navigate the narrow ledge. The air smelled bad. That was something Snake hadn't noticed in his out-of-body excursion into the cave. It wasn't bad enough to make them sick, but it was a stale odor that assaulted the senses of people used to living in the open air.

Across the cavern, on the other side of the river, a huge waterfall poured down, making it difficult for the men to hear each other.

Deer called out, "How far is it now, Shaman?"

Snake answered with a wave of his hand, "Just around that bend ahead."

They continued to inch along, and finally made it around the large stalactite in their path. Eagle said, "I hope she is capable of walking. It would be hard to carry a dead weight around this pillar."

Snake said loudly, "She was awake and moving when I saw her."

Doorway Series:
Morning Star Rises

He looked down at the river and then wished he hadn't. The feeling in the pit of his stomach made him feel sick. It was funny, he thought, that his out-of-body trips didn't elicit this response, but when he was in his body, he had a fear of heights.

As Snake moved along the ledge, he could see small lights darting above the river. The people believed that the caves were openings to the Underworld, and they came into caves to speak to their departed relatives and to honor the gods. When he had been in this cave, searching, in his spirit form, for Mesquite, he saw the lights as small water spirits. He decided he would have to check into this at another time; because, at the moment, his focus was on keeping a firm footing on the slippery ledge.

Luckily, their path widened as they came around the enormous stalactite. Through the dim light from a small opening overhead, they could barely make out Mesquite's form. She appeared to be sleeping.

As Snake neared the reclining form, he saw that she had, indeed, lost consciousness. She lay with her mouth open—still tied hand and foot, as she had been. He could see her chest move shallowly with her breath. He looked around. Yes, the fire pit was as he had seen it, and the writing on the walls. He hadn't noticed the altar rock that he now saw nearby.

He turned to his friends and shouted, "She is alive!"

Kneeling down, he cut through her bonds with his small knife. Mesquite opened her eyes, and flinched in fear. She squatted, rubbing her wrists and ankles where the bonds had been tight, and shivered.

Eagle and Deer stood apart and watched.

Snake, still kneeling, sheathed his knife. He looked into Mesquite's eyes as if searching for something. Finally, his voice gentle, he said, "You live, Sister."

The burn marks on her arms and legs had begun to fester.

Doorway Series:
Morning Star Rises

Snake said, "Soldiers, has either of you carried your healing salve with you?"

Deer pulled a small packet from his belt and handed it to Snake. "I have some, Shaman."

Snake took the salve, and dipping his finger in, reached out to apply it to Mesquite's burns.

She flinched with a whimper, but said nothing.

He said, "This will soothe your burns. It will not hurt."

Mesquite forced herself to sit still as he reached out to her again. The fight had gone out of her, but she had no reason to trust that these men wouldn't assault her. She had heard stories of Aztec soldiers. It was said that they cared for the physical needs of their captives, and sometimes even treated them to fine living and feasting—until the time they would sacrifice them. She waited, believing they would eventually kill her, and she accepted her fate.

Snake gave Mesquite a drink of fresh water and told her to stand and move about. She had lain so long in the cave that her muscles were stiff and her legs felt numb. As she walked and stretched, she started to feel stronger.

Eagle saw that she was more limber, and he said, "She looks able to make the trip back, Shaman. It is getting late. Can we leave now?"

Snake answered, "Yes, Lord."

He turned to Mesquite and said, "This way is hard. We must go along a narrow ledge for part of the way. I am going to tie a tether between us in case you grow weak. We don't want you to fall in the river."

Mesquite still didn't trust them, but she accepted that they were the captors—and besides, what choice did she have? What did she have left? She held out both her hands, but was surprised when the Shaman ignored her hands and tied a tether around her waist and then his. A small doubt began to insinuate itself in her mind—perhaps these men weren't pretending, she thought. Perhaps they really were what they appeared to be. She dismissed this thought as quickly as she recognized it.

The trip back seemed to take forever, winding through the various caverns after finally alighting from the ledge alongside the river. It was a relief to all of them to crawl out into the open air. They didn't realize it had taken them so long inside; the sun was about to go down as they shinnied their way up a vine behind the small clump of bushes that hid the cave opening.

The cave had been chilly and damp, smelling slightly of sulfur. Mesquite was worn out. She started to climb the vine but didn't have the strength, so Eagle went up to the top and dropped down a vine. Deer tied it around her waist, and followed her up. Half climbing, and half pushed by Deer and pulled by Eagle, she finally made it to the top. As she reached the plateau, she fell forward, crawled a little way, and lay in a crumpled ball.

***

When Mesquite finally awoke, she smelled meat cooking over a fire before she opened her eyes. Then she noticed the sun was warm on her body, and her burns didn't hurt anymore. She peered through almost closed eyes to see what was happening.

"The food is ready to eat," Snake said. He had spent several years cooking for Deer's household, and then for the group of travelers on the trail. He naturally fell into the roll of the cook, even now when he was a Shaman, and no longer a slave. Mesquite didn't know about his former life, and couldn't believe the Shaman would be cooking for the others. She opened her eyes all the way and sat up.

Eagle glanced at her and said, "Good, she is awake in time to eat before we leave."

Mesquite sat up and was surprised to discover that she wasn't tied up. She couldn't figure out what their game was.

Doorway Series:
Morning Star Rises

"Come and eat!" Snake held out a stick of savory meat. The smell almost overwhelmed Mesquite. Still, she was afraid—too afraid to reach for the food.

Seeing her hesitancy, Snake gestured with the stick of meat. "Come, eat! We must be on the trail soon. You need the meat. It will give you strength."

Mesquite knew the truth of his remark, and she forced herself to stand, walk over to him, and take the stick. Unable to hold back any longer, she tore at the meat with her teeth, barely chewing before she swallowed. She finished before the men even started. Snake handed her another stick of meat, and she devoured that one, too. Then she realized there were only four sticks of meat. Without a word, the three men shared the remaining meat, put out the fire, and set out on the trail.

Mesquite watched them as they walked away.

***

The Celebration of Oneness had come to an end. On the previous day, the entire Royal Family was in the Plaza. Lined up in their best regalia, including the children by their sides, they stood for hours as they said farewell to their new friends and allies.

Now, in the stillness of early morning, the Royal Family walked up the steps of the high pyramid to the temple at the top, overlooking the city. Only the sounds of the birds, wildlife and the soft breeze accompanied them on their way. Reaching the summit, they looked out at the City of the Door between Heaven and Earth. Before turning to enter the temple of the One, they watched the sky. In the pre-dawn, before the rising of the sun, they saw what they searched for. There it was—the promise that they would not be alone—the Morning Star! They knew that the path of their destiny still beckoned to them.

PART THREE

The wise man a light, a torch, a stout torch
that does not smoke;
A perforated mirror, a mirror pierced on both sides.
His are the black and red ink, his are the illustrated
manuscripts...
He himself is writing and wisdom.
He is the path, the true way for others.[7]

1

Tawny with black spots, muscles tensed in the strong hind legs, the large male jaguar watched the movement below the high branch he was perched on. Green-brown eyes narrowed. Tail twitched. The large ruby colored stone hanging from a leather thong around his neck began to grow warm as it nestled against his chest.

He watched the young woman below. Long blue-black hair gently moved against the golden skin of her back. She slipped among the trees, careful to not make a sound. Her attention caught by a pair of hummingbirds, she was drawn to the flowered bush where they hovered. Quietly, ever so quietly, her lean brown legs carried her toward them. She stopped and held her breath as she watched the sacred birds. Suddenly turning her head, she gazed up at the jaguar, blue fire dancing in her eyes as she spotted him.

It was a game they had played for years. Her win secured, she turned her back on him. Bending over the rounded bush, she looked intently at the small lavender trumpet-shaped flowers, while inhaling the heady fragrance. She seemed to be lost in the beauty, the jaguar in the tree apparently having slipped from her mind.

The jaguar leaped from the branch, landing soundlessly on the forest floor. He concentrated on the stone about his neck and it began to vibrate and glow. He rose from the ground, upright on two legs, and sneaked up behind the girl. Grabbing her around the waist, he said, "How do you manage to do that, Little One?"

Feather turned her head and looked at him over her shoulder.

"Oh, Jaguar, it is so easy! How many times over the years now have I told you that we are Spirit Twins? Of course I can always find you!"

Jaguar didn't answer. She pulled away from him and turned around. His familiar face still made her heart beat faster. Her blue gaze, like a caress on his skin, moved down to his smooth brown shoulders, his tattooed chest, arms and legs. She glanced up at his face again.

"My womanhood celebration will fall on the new moon," she said proudly. "I am ready to marry. Now, I must find a suitable husband. Do you know of anyone?"

Feather smiled with tender amusement at Jaguar's consternation. Even though he was six years older than she, he sometimes acted like a naive child. Gone were the days when her boyhood friend tried to hide from her as she relentlessly followed him everywhere. The day had finally come when he started looking at her as a woman, rather than the childish nuisance he had considered her for some time. Still, he seemed to be tongue-tied when things got serious.

"What would the Queen say if she knew what you were doing?" he asked.

Feather answered, "The Queen would say, 'How wise of you, my daughter. Jaguar is the only one who will make you a worthy husband.'"

She looked defiantly at him. "Must you pretend with me, Brother? You know that we are both grown and that, as the Queen's daughter, I must have a mate. You are far past the time when most young men think about such things. Has your vocation as a Shaman/Healer sapped your strength? Have you no manly needs?"

Jaguar looked stricken. He pulled away from Feather and quickly disappeared through the trees. Head lowered, she turned back to the City, warm tears clouding her vision. She was furious and confused. Torn between her hurt pride and wounded heart, she felt the need to talk to an older woman.

She decided to talk to the Priestess, Morning Star. Perhaps this wise woman would be able to help her understand what was going on with Jaguar. She, too, was a Shaman/Healer so perhaps she would have some insight into Jaguar's strange behavior.

Feather had left the Priestess shortly before playing the seeking game with Jaguar. All morning, the Priestess had been quizzing her on her knowledge. Feather, a day away from her womanhood celebration, was at the end of her formal education. It had been arduous, but Feather had a brilliant mind.

Her education had begun the moment she was born, just before her family entered the new city of Ilhuicatl for the first time. Ilhuicatl meant "The Door." The Priestess taught her that Ilhuicatl was the door between heaven and earth. This meant that it was a power place, where the veil between the worlds was thin.

Feather's childhood had been filled with stories about the long journey to find this city. Her first memory was of the little boy Jaguar, telling her the stories. He enjoyed teaching his younger friend—until he decided he couldn't be bothered by the adoring little girl. But Feather had her own activities so she didn't mind so much that Jaguar thought she was a pest. While he was in the school for priests or spending days in the forest, she had her studies with the Priestess, the Queen, and others. She was a natural student and wanted to know everything.

Impatiently rubbing the tears from her eyes, Feather remembered how excited she had been the first time she was praised for her scribing. She loved painting the glyphs and learning all the lore behind them. Each glyph represented a whole world of understanding. It was as if there were different levels of knowledge within the written language, just as there were within the oral stories of the

Singers. She loved the mathematics, as she gradually evolved into an understanding of how everything—the All—was based on, and existed by and through, the mathematical functions. Music was the same, each tone representing and encompassing the energies of the Creator. But closest to her heart were the astronomy/astrology, and the histories—especially the more recent history of her extended family on their long journey.

Feather never tired of hearing how her mother, Mockingbird, and her auntie, Morning Star, had been prophesied to be the Enlightened Leaders of a new society—and how this had come true. It had been fulfilled because of the dedication, belief and trust of the people who aided them: the legendary High Priestess, Tlacotl, who had given her life for her Queen; the large-hearted nursery caregiver, Singer, who also died on the path; Flower and Deer, parents to Jaguar; her Uncle, Snake, who had become a Shaman, and husband to the Priestess; and most of all, her wonderful father and Consort to her mother, Eagle.

All of the lessons were interwoven with the Law of One—the spiritual tenet that there was one Creator, and that all were a part of that One. She knew this as a tiny child, and had never lost her connections with Spirit, even though she sometimes let her will try to control things. As an infant, Feather could hear and see things that many others could not—the wonderful Spirits that guided her—and her abilities continued to grow in the nurturing community of Ihuicatl.

Still, in this moment, Feather was very much a human woman. Her heart ached at the rejection.

***

Deep in the forest on the other side of the city of Ilhuicatl, Jaguar, in human form, sat on a branch bent low from a lightning strike months before. One leg bent at the knee, foot resting on the branch, while the other swung back and forth a couple inches from the ground. The green rain forest, teeming with life, was a mere backdrop to his inner turmoil.

He knew that Feather felt hurt and angry with him, but he didn't know how to make it right. She thought he was rejecting her love—he knew that. He didn't know how to explain to her that it was precisely because he loved her so much that he couldn't wed her. Years before, when he had used his healing power to bring her back to her body, he had gone into the dream and joined his spirit with hers, and he had seen her destiny. He knew that she didn't remember and that he would never forget.

2

Shell stood on the shore, signaling to her husband, Net. She could see the twins swimming near the boat. Son and daughter, they were born after months of discomfort for Shell. Now in their fifth year, the children frolicked in the sea just as their father had before them. He had started them swimming before they could walk, for fear that they might wander away from their mother while she was busy at her work. She remembered how astonished she had been when he walked out into the sea with a baby under each arm. Astonishment turned to fear when he placed them in the water and turned to her with a huge smile on his sun-browned face.

"Look, my wife! Look at our children!"

Water dripping from his hair, Net laughed as his twin son and daughter disappeared under the sea beside him.

Shell screamed, "What have you done?"

She ran to the shore and out into the sea to save her children. Thinking she would retrieve two frightened choking babies from the water, she pushed against Net's chest with both her hands, and he fell with a splash. Frantically, she searched for the children.

"It's all right, Wife. It's all right." He tried to soothe her with his voice.

Then, he reached down and lifted one dripping child up and then the other. Shell dropped her jaw in amazement as the babies gurgled and laughed. They weren't choking nor gasping for breath. They were happy and safe.

Shell began to cry as she reached for her tiny naked children.

Net said, "Hush. You will frighten them. They have been swimming with me for two days now. Your children are at home in the sea, my wife!"

He handed his daughter to Shell and carried his son under his arm as they waded back to shore.

When Shell thought about it now, she still could vaguely feel the panic she had felt then for her babies, but she now knew they were safe with Net. He took them to the sea while they were babies so they would never learn to fear water. That had been in their first summer. Now, in their fifth summer, they swam like fish, but Net always kept a close eye on them. She no longer panicked because she knew the wisdom of what he had done.

Net waved at her and called to his children to come to the canoe. He saw the men standing on the shore with his wife, and he was excited that they had come. It was the men from the City of Ilhuicatl, and he hadn't seen them for a long time. Hurriedly, he pulled the canoe into shore, lifted out his children, and greeted his old friends.

"Welcome, welcome, my dear friends. It has been too long! My wife and I were just speaking of you this morning, and of how we desired to make a trip to the city to visit you."

Eagle said, "Yes, it is good. You both look well, and your children are growing so rapidly. I could not believe my eyes when I saw them diving under the water beside your boat! How well they swim!"

Net said, "Come. Come to our calli and we will eat. You are probably in need of food and rest after your journey!"

With a grin lighting his face, he and Shell led the way to their home. The children ran to join a group of friends who were playing with a ball.

As they walked through the village, they stopped to chat with several people. In this small village, everyone knew who the visitors were. All but the youngest had been to the city of Ilhuicatl for the Great Celebration of Oneness ten years previously. Stories were still told about this great event. Many had been there often, some going to the market on a regular basis with their wares, foods, and arts. The city had become a big trading center, and something was always going on. It was a chance to visit with relatives or get news of those who had married out of the village. The Temple of Education was there, and some of the children were sent to the city for school. They would bring what they had learned back to their villages and would become the teachers of the next generations.

Eagle noticed a bony woman squatting on the ground in front of a calli. She was tracing a pattern in the sand with a stick. A tall, skinny, younger man called her inside, but she just stared at the ground as if she didn't hear him. She looked vaguely familiar to Eagle. Then he remembered—it was Mesquite! The last time Eagle had seen her was when they rescued her from the cave where someone had imprisoned her in preparation for a sacrifice! Eagle, Deer, and Snake had set her loose, and hadn't seen her since.

He said quietly, "Net, is that Mesquite over there?"

Net said, "Yes, Lord."

Snake said, "She looks like one whose soul has departed."

Shell said, "That is all she does. She sits there and traces designs in the sand. She doesn't answer to anyone anymore. Not since the Festival of Oneness, many years ago."

Net said, "She showed up about a week after the Festival. She was dirty and bruised, her clothing torn and burned. I know I hadn't seen her since she had her men tie me to a tree. Then the sky rained fire and the earth opened up. You and your soldiers came to find me, and I didn't see Mesquite again until she came back to the village. She hasn't really spoken since that time except to make strange sounds. It is as if she doesn't remember anything. She wouldn't even eat if her son, Zolin, didn't hand-feed her."

Shell said, "And sometimes, my Auntie Magnolia watches her if Zolin has work to do."

Soon, the visitors were gathered around the fire with Net and Shell, eating and laughing and catching up on all the news. Finally, the time had come to extend the invitation.

Eagle said, "My friends, as you know, long ago the Queen welcomed you into our family. You are as our own blood. If it were not for your love of the sea and your village, we would have asked you to live with us in the city; but we realized that would have been selfish on our part, and you may have found it difficult to refuse. Your visits have always been received with joy, and we would ask you to make another such visit. We ask you to attend the womanhood celebration of our daughter, Feather."

Shell clapped her hands in joy.

Net replied, "Uncle, this is a great honor! Of course we will come."

Shell asked, "When is the ceremony, Uncle?"

Eagle said, "In four days time. Will you be able to leave tomorrow?"

Net said, "We will! It will be good for the children to go along. They will meet everyone we have told them about, and see the wonders of the great city!"

With that settled, Shell busied herself preparing for the journey, and Net went to find his children.

Snake said, "I have been thinking about the woman, Mesquite. I will talk to her son."

3

Zolin looked up from his loom and he saw the
Shaman approach. He had last seen him in the city during
the Festival of Oneness so many years before. Zolin
watched him, trying to understand what was so memorable
about this rather short muscular man. Zolin knew he was a
healer and that he was the consort to the lovely Priestess,
Morning Star. The Shaman hadn't changed much; but he
looked a little more confident than he had then. He had the
same generous mouth, large soft-brown eyes and a head of
full thick hair, now streaked with areas of gray amidst the
black.
    Zolin wondered what it was about this man that had
drawn the Priestess to him. He wasn't especially handsome
or remarkable in any way; to the contrary, he looked quite
ordinary. As the Shaman neared, Zolin saw that he looked
more mature but wasn't lined in the face, and he walked
with ease. As someone who had always felt inferior
physically, Zolin noticed these things.
    He felt his heart race as the Shaman drew near.
Memories of his part in his mother's mad plan to destroy
the City Royal House flashed through his mind, and he was
afraid, but he stood to face his fate. In a way, he felt relief.
For ten years he had just barely lived, trying to care for the
mindless woman in his calli, learning a trade to support
them, and knowing the unspoken thoughts of the villagers
who tolerated their presence. He was an outcast from his
society, even though this was never said aloud nor made
official with any type of ceremony. It was inherent in the
fact that he never forgave himself, and he saw his place in

life through his own distorted vision. Unable to forgive himself, he was sure that no one else forgave him either. As he stood before the Shaman of Ilhuicatl, he was ready to accept his punishment.

Snake said, "You do fine work on the loom, Weaver. The pattern is beautiful, and the colors are very bright."

Zolin answered, "Thank you, Lord. I am but a clumsy weaver, not born to it."

"You are Zolin, son of Mesquite and Wolf, are you not?"

"Yes, Lord."

"And your mother is a widow, is that correct?"

"Yes, Lord."

"I am Snake, Consort to the Priestess of Ilhuicatl, and Shaman/Teacher in the Temple of Healing."

"Yes, Lord. I know of you. I am honored by your presence. Can I offer you food or drink?"

"Thank you, but I just ate, Weaver. I would dispense of the proprieties for the sake of necessity. Our time here in the village is short. We are leaving in the morning."

"Certainly, Shaman. Speak your mind."

"Very well, Weaver. How is your mother?"

"Truth to tell, Shaman, her health appears to be good, but she may as well have died. Truly, when her body came back to the village after the earthquake so long ago, her spirit did not follow. I don't know where she was for those several days after the quake. One day, she walked into the village like a woman in a dream, as though she didn't know where she was. She was bruised and dirty, her clothing burned and torn, and her power necklace was gone. She spoke a few words when she arrived, but she has remained silent ever since."

Zolin's description brought the clear memory back to Snake. He remembered how they had delivered Mesquite from the sacrificial cave. She went with them willingly, but as though she was drained of purpose. They had fed her and let her sleep the night under their protection. He could picture her as they left—sitting by herself, watching them depart as if she couldn't quite believe it. He wondered now if they should have taken her back to the city with them, even though she had tried unsuccessfully to destroy everything they had built. But, at the time, they thought they were setting her free to find her way home. They thought they were doing what was best for her in allowing her to follow her will.

Snake silently reminisced for a few moments, and then he was moved to ask, "Tell me, Zolin, were you able to understand what she said? Do you recall her words?"

Zolin said, "Yes, Lord. The words haunt me in my dreams. I have been unable to get her to speak since that day. But it wasn't like she was speaking to me. She talked as if a thought just came out of her mouth, and she didn't even know it. She said, 'I wasn't good enough for them or their gods. They left me, too.'"

Snake said, "Do you know the meaning of her words?"

"No, Shaman."

"I think I do, Zolin."

"Can you tell me, Shaman?"

"I will tell you what I know, and also what I surmise, Zolin. On the day after that earthquake, I found Mesquite in the mouth of Mother Earth, in a cave—an underground river. She was tied up at an altar, and left alone. There were bones there in the ashes of an old fire, and many items of beauty stashed in a recess in the wall. I am not sure why she was left there alone. It looked as though she was going to be sacrificed in the land of the dead, but no one else was near.

The soldiers who are here with me now went with me and we released her from her bonds. We helped her to escape her imprisonment. She seemed to feel that she was our prisoner. When we left her the next morning to return to the City, she did not seem to realize she had been freed."

Zolin said, "But who would have taken her to the cave? Who would do such a thing?"

"I don't know, Zolin, but I do know it wasn't the soldiers of the City. Now, this is what I surmise—I believe that she felt we would take her to be used as a sacrifice in the City. I believe she accepted that it was her fate, and that it was honorable and just. When we left her to go free, I believe she felt it was because we found her unworthy. I want you to know, Zolin, that our One God does not demand nor accept such a sacrifice from us. The only acceptable sacrifice is the sacrifice of our selfish ways."

Zolin thought about this. Then he said, "What you have said about my mother is probably true. It fits with the way she seemed to believe the world works."

Snake said, "And you, Zolin? Does it fit with your beliefs?"

Zolin said, "I used to believe everything my mother told me. I wanted to believe her because she was my mother. Since then, I have had much time to consider these things for myself. I have little contact with others, but I watch and listen and learn. Without my mother to give me the meaning of things, I am free to discover on my own. I am a man now, and a man should think for himself."

"And what have you learned?"

Zolin said, "I have learned that my mother had many misconceptions."

The two men sat in silence for some time.

Finally, Snake said, "Weaver...Zolin...do you give me leave to see if I can help her?"

Zolin answered, "There is nothing to lose, Shaman. She has no life now. If her body perishes, there still is nothing to lose. I am her son, Shaman, and I know she did love me."

Doorway Series:
Morning Star Rises

Eagle and Deer watched from shore as Net's large
trading canoe was being loaded. When Net's father, the
Trader, had died, Net spent a season building the canoe. It
was a creation of magnificence, large and swift. It was
stable and waterproof. Up to six men could paddle it, but
usually only two went, loaded down with trading goods
from the village. The men purchased the goods from the
villagers to sell in other lands and paid Net a portion of
their profits for the use of the canoe on their return.

The arrangement suited everyone well; most of all,
it suited Net. The canoe rent, on top of the income from his
net making and repair allowed him to stay in the village he
loved so dearly. It was especially important for Net to be
with his family and to swim with the dolphins. He had told
Deer how lonely his mother had been when his father was
gone for extended periods of time on his trade route.
Sometimes his father had been gone for a year or
more—and the Aztec soldiers had even taken him captive
one time. If it hadn't been for Deer, he and his mother may
never have seen his father again.

At that time, Deer had been a high Aztec soldier in
charge of a troop of men. It happened that Deer and his
men came upon another troop of soldiers who had
wrongfully imprisoned Net's father. Deer forced the other
soldiers to let Turtle go, and Net's father had never
forgotten the debt he owed to the soldier.

That had been long ago. When the men once again
met several years after that event, Net's father saw an
opportunity to help the soldier. Deer had been among those
who aided the Enlightened Leaders in their escape from the
Temple Priests.

As the giant canoe pulled smoothly away from
shore, the men watched it out of sight, and then went back
toward Net's calli. Deer saw Snake in the distance. He sat
on the ground, facing Mesquite. She appeared to be
unaware that he was there as she squatted in her usual

position, scratching something on the ground with a stick. Snake didn't appear disturbed by this. He sat silently and waited.

***

In the Shaman's mind, it was no longer silent. He had entered into Mesquite's reality. It had been a long search to find an opening into the chaos. The small aperture had shifted every time he felt close. Finally, he jumped before it moved, and found himself in a deep quagmire of grey. The fog was so thick it threatened to swallow him. Balls of fire fell from above, narrowly missing him. He felt/heard a deep rumbling and he fell into a never-ending hole. Rivers of fire rained down, surrounding him. Evil things loomed in the darkness, waiting to pounce. He knew he was in the mind of the mad woman.

Snake fought to remember who he was and why he was here. It was difficult. He forced himself to find a landing, and finally caught onto a ledge. Pulling himself up, he strained to see into the darkness. Ah...a weak flickering light was ahead. He pulled himself to his feet, and then found he had to crawl on his belly to fit into the small cave-like opening. As he moved forward, the light grew a little brighter...he searched for Mesquite.

Suddenly, there she was...singing a mournful song...moving her arms in graceful arcs as the light traced patterns on the cave walls. The patterns formed into the same designs she had traced in the sand.

He spoke to her, "Mesquite...Mesquite...do you hear me?"

Slowly, she turned with a strange smile. Her sudden scream seemed to pierce him like a knife, and he fell backwards, out of the light and back into the deep fog. He tried to walk, but he slipped on the slime beneath his feet.

The Shaman began to chant: "Mesquite. Sister. Child of the Great One...you are not alone." From within a deep well of compassion, love flowed out of him into the grey fog, searching for the lost woman. A faint light appeared and the ground became solid. He saw her ahead of him with her back turned, and he increased the flow of love. "You are not alone. You are never alone. You are a part of the One."

***

The next morning when Zolin woke, the first thing he saw was that his mother was not in her bed. Rushing from the calli, he was met by a strange sight. His mother stood in the midst of several women of the village. They spoke softly and soothingly to her, as if she were a lost child—calming and reassuring. Zolin was confused. Even in health, his mother had never a part of the community of women. She had always been apart, angry and sullen.

Then, Mesquite lifted her eyes to Zolin, dry tears streaking her cheeks. Her ravaged face softened as she said, "My son!"

4

Ten year-old Light was with the Priestess, when Feather found her. For a moment, she forgot about her own plight as she watched the mother and son from the doorway. Morning Star leaned towards Light as they talked. Feather could see her excitement; so she stood quietly, not wanting to interrupt.

"Mother," Light said, "it will be soon. I was told this."

"How soon, Son?"

"I don't know exactly, Mother; but I was told that we are almost ready!"

Morning Star leaned back with a small satisfied sigh. Then she sensed Feather standing in the doorway. Turning her head, she gave Feather a welcoming smile and reached out her hand to gesture her in.

Feather said, "I do not want to intrude, Auntie. I can come back later if it's more convenient."

Morning Star said, "Come in, Child. My son and I are through for the moment. He is doing extremely well in his studies. The student has surpassed the teacher!"

With a fond look at her son, Morning Star told him, "You may go now, Light. You need some time with your friends."

Rising, he said, "Thank you, Mother."

He turned to Feather with a smile and said, "Tomorrow is your ceremony! Put a smile on your face, Big Sister. All will be well!"

After Light left, Morning Star said, "Now, Feather, seat yourself here next to me." She patted the bench. "Let us talk."

Doorway Series:
Morning Star Rises

***

Light didn't feel like finding his friends. He needed time alone to ponder all that was happening. He knew things that many of the others weren't aware of, and it confused him. Why should he know these things? He could talk to his parents about it but his mother was so busy, and his father was at the fishing village.

He decided to go exploring in the caverns beneath the palace. Some of the tunnels were flooded now, since the Queen had been locked down there. He knew that there was another entrance than the one Mockingbird had used, and it wasn't flooded. It was damp; caused, his father said, by the underground river that had flown through there. It had somehow been diverted into the caverns that led to the hidden treasury. They still didn't know for sure how it had happened. Mockingbird had said that she believed it was her fault. She told about how she had been so thirsty that she dug into the soft damp stone wall with her knife, hoping to find enough moisture to wet her mouth. She said the water had eventually worn a large hole in the wall, and the water come rushing through. Everyone had been warned to stay out of the caverns; but, something called to Light from deep within the earth.

He remembered the way. His father, Snake, had found the entrance a few years before. It was hidden well, but his father had a way of leaving his body to search things out. He hadn't done it purposely, but was drawn there while in meditation. Light knew that something was in the cavern waiting for him.

Now that his mind was made up, Light wished his cousin, Jaguar, was with him. Even though Jaguar was a man now, he always treated Light as an equal. He could talk to him about anything, and Jaguar always seemed to understand. Feather was his friend, too, but she had a way of mothering him, and he didn't want a mother just now. Anyway, she needed to prepare for her womanhood ceremony—and she had been crying last he saw her, so she wouldn't be in any mood to go on an exploration with him.

Light knew the hidden entrance could be reached from inside the Temple of Education. His father had shown him once, but they didn't go very far into it. He walked through the massive halls, empty today of the usual bustle of people. Most days, there were classes going on, groups in discussion, and lone students doing research. Today was different because of Feather's upcoming womanhood ceremony. The Queen had declared a full period of thirteen days in which to get ready for the celebration. She was the first daughter of the Royal Family, and this called for much preparation.

Now, Light released the catch to the opening, lit a torch, and entered. It was cold in the tunnel, but Light was so excited that he didn't notice. The farther he walked, the more he felt the pull of something waiting in the shadows. It wasn't anything to fear; to the contrary, he knew it was something he wanted to find. The tunnel appeared to go deeper and deeper into Mother Earth, until it abruptly ended.

He held his torch with one hand; and with the other, he felt along the walls. He searched and searched, but could not find an opening. In frustration, he shouted, "You have called me down here—now, show me the way!"

He stepped back and held the torch high over his head. Suddenly, Light saw the inscription carved high on the wall: In lak ech—You are my other self!

5

Mockingbird rose from her intricately carved throne. She had just finished with the last petitioner for the day. It had been a simple case, involving damaged goods and how best the wrongdoer could repair the harm. Several pottery containers were broken in a merchant's booth because a child ran into them when he was running away from another child. The miscreant and the parents representing him had used the argument that it was an accident—a whim of fate—and the child shouldn't be held liable. The decision of the monarch required a fine of 60 cocoa beans to be paid by the parents of the youth to the merchant. She added a further fine of 120 cocoa beans to be paid by the parents of the youth who chased the first child. The merchant was satisfied. Mockingbird knew that the parents who had to pay the fines were well able to do so; and they would chastise the children involved, and teach them that there were consequences to their behavior.

The boys lived at the school, and they would also be required by their teachers to learn the craft of pottery making. They would work at it for as long as it took to make at least one piece of good everyday ware, and this would teach them the value of the labor of the potter.

Mockingbird thought, *Who knows? Perhaps they will like it so well that we will have two new potters in the City!*

She went to her private apartment in the palace to change out of her formal clothing, and then to her private garden. As she thought about the next day's festivities, she felt a mixture of happiness and sadness. Her daughter was a woman now, and they would mark the occasion with a great feast, with music and dance. It would be memorable—the first daughter of the royal family to reach womanhood in the city. Still, Feather was Mockingbird's only child, and it was difficult for her to think of her taking on the responsibilities of a woman.

To her surprise, Feather was in the garden already. She and Morning Star were seated on a bench, talking. Mockingbird could see that Feather had been crying. Startled, she rushed to her side and took her in her arms.

"What is it, Little One?"

Holding Feather to her chest and rocking her comfortingly, she looked over her head at Morning Star. Star said nothing, waiting for Feather to answer her mother.

Finally, Feather composed herself and pulled back. "It is nothing, Nantli...nothing you can help."

Mockingbird thought, *I am supposed to be wise enough to help everyone in the city...but my own daughter I cannot help. I have to allow her to work it out herself. It isn't easy being a leader.*

6

Jaguar recalled the vision he had experienced after he had healed Feather. Even though it had been ten years before, when he and Feather were both children, the memory was as clear as if it had been the previous day.

She was such a tiny child, lying on the ground and wrapped in a blanket. Her face was ashen and she was so still, he thought at first that her spirit had fled. He remembered how desperately he had pleaded for her life as he tried to channel healing energy into her frail form. He was only eight years old at the time, and had only healed one time before, when he had killed the cougar. That had been spontaneous and he didn't even realize what he was doing. He only knew that he had taken a life, and he had to give it back.

Feather had finally opened those startling blue eyes and looked at him with adoration. Then, she fell asleep and he knew she was healed. Her little face had regained its color and her breathing was even. He was relieved, and suddenly realized how ravenous he was.

Later that evening, as they rested around the fire, Jaguar was almost asleep. As he lay in rest, he began to see pictures of the future. It frightened him so much that he couldn't speak of it. Now, it was time. He had to talk to the Shaman. He had to talk to Uncle Snake.

***

The party from the fishing village was met with much joking, talk, laughter, and feasting. The twins were in awe of the magnificent city. After hours of visiting and catching up on all the news, the visitors were shown to their quarters. Snake and Morning Star were alone together when Jaguar arrived.

"Auntie and Uncle," he began. "I would speak with you both about something of the greatest importance. I realize it is late and I wouldn't bother you, but it is something that cannot wait."

Morning Star said, "Enter, Jaguar. We have been waiting for you."

"Then you know what I shall say?"

Snake laughed gently and said, "No, Son, but we know that it involves Feather."

Jaguar said, "But how do you know?"

Morning Star answered, "Jaguar, Feather spoke with me today. She was very confused. She loves you and believes you love her; but she said that you will not speak of marriage. Was she mistaken? Perhaps we should call her in and all talk together?"

Jaguar said, "Please, no. Not yet. I have something I would like to tell you about first."

The elders waited for Jaguar to go on.

Finally, he began to tell them of the vision he had so many years ago, that had caused him such great fear. "I saw Feather as a woman, and I knew that we were wed. She was in labor with our son. It was all so real, I am sure it was a true vision. It was terrible." He paused, a look of pain ravaging his face.

Snake gently prodded him, "Go on."

"In my vision, Feather was in terrible pain. It went on and on. In the end, she died, along with our son. There—it is said—after all of these years."

Jaguar paced, unable to contain his agony. "So, you see, I cannot marry Feather. I cannot be the cause of her death! And I cannot tell her this!"

Morning Star put her arm around Jaguar's shoulders. Both she and her husband loved this boy, and knew what a good heart he had.

Doorway Series:
Morning Star Rises

She said, "Jaguar, both my husband and I have received many visions, and know something of them. The first I ever had was terrifying. It was when Mockingbird and I were servers in the temple in Tenochtitlan, the Aztec capitol. My vision showed me that both Mockingbird and I would be sacrificed to the sun god, Huitzilopochtli! It was so real, and so clear, Jaguar. I was so frightened! Then, the High Priestess Tlacotl explained something to me. She said that sometimes we are given visions of things that can happen so that we can make changes. Sometimes we can use them as a tool to change our course. Finally, I understood that having a vision did not always mean that this event had to occur. The Priestess knew of the prophecy of Quetzalcoatl about the two who would create a new destiny. She helped us, that night, to escape from the temple. You remember her from our long journey here to the City of the Door. It wouldn't have happened at all if we had just accepted the vision as pre-determined and stayed to await our fate!

"The reason I am telling you this, Jaguar, is so that you will know that you don't have to accept the fate you saw in your vision. My husband is a great healer. He can work with Feather to see if there is a problem that can be healed. If not, I was taught about herbs that keep a woman from getting pregnant. You do not have to accept such sadness, Jaguar. This dream vision was a gift from Spirit to help you to realize your happiness."

At this moment, ten-year-old Light burst into the room.

"Mother! Father! I have found it!"

Snake said, "Son, Can you not see that we are talking with your cousin? What have you discovered that makes you forget to be polite?"

Light said, "Oh, forgive me, but I cannot wait! And you will want to know, too, Jaguar!"

Feeling some relief, Jaguar was amused by Light. He said, "You show such excitement, young cousin! What have you found?"

"I have found the opening to the Great Library! The library of the Old Ones! I couldn't believe it! I have never seen so many books, Mother! Come! Come and see it!"

***

The news was too great to wait until morning. Mockingbird and Eagle were almost asleep when Morning Star was announced. The others waited until Morning Star explained to the Queen and her Consort what Light had discovered. Immediately, they rose from bed and sent for their daughter to join them.

Jaguar's face lit up when they came out with Feather. He smiled at her and saw the joy in her eyes.

Light led the way as the entire party followed him into the Temple of Education and into the subterranean levels. He had closed the door before leaving, and he now stopped in front of it. His heart raced with excitement as he turned and said, "This is it!"

A series of maneuvers were performed by the boy, and finally, the door slid open. He entered and stood aside, holding his torch high, as the rest followed. A gasp echoed throughout the vault as the others became aware of the magnitude of the immense library. Stone ledges on the walls contained thousands of covered containers.

"I opened several containers," said Light, as he held up a book. "This is what I found—some of leather and some made from leaves of gold! They are books! The knowledge of the Old Ones! And look!" He walked to the center of the cavern, where the others joined him.

"I couldn't lift this lid. It is too heavy."

A large stone sarcophagus stood in the center of the room. As the others crowded around, he said, "When I came to the door and read the inscription, I remembered being here before! I was the one who ordered the inscription to be carved above the doorway! Can it be true, Nantli?" he asked his mother.

Morning Star, with her vast understanding of the things of Spirit, said, "Yes, my Son! It is true. Tell me, Light, do you remember what is in the sarcophagus? Oh, there is writing on the lid—look!"

She read, "Here lies the gift of the Morning Star."

Mockingbird said, "Oh Sister, we thought we had lost so much when the treasury was flooded, but just look what we have gained! The river must have gone past this vault to hide it until the time was right! This library is a glorious gift, worth so much more than jewels and statuary, and we have so much to learn from the contents! Are we to open the sarcophagus, Little Sister? It is for you to decide."

Morning Star said, "I believe we are to open it or we would not be here."

Mockingbird said, "Then, perhaps the men are able to lift the lid. Do you wish for them to try it now?"

"Yes, now! I won't be able to sleep with wondering what lies beneath it! I don't hold all the memories of Quetzalcoatl—only some which come at their own time. I know no more than the rest of you what this chest holds."

Feather said, "I will hold your torch, Little Brother."

Each male took a corner of the lid and were able to lift it with great strain. Finally, they were able to slide it to the floor. Feather held the torch over the opening, and they were amazed to see another cask inside—this one covered in gold. On the lid, a relief projected from the surface. It held the face of a man—one with wavy hair and a beard. The Shaman said in a hushed voice, "The face of the Prophet!"

Upon seeing the face of Quetzalcoatl adorning the small casket of gold, Morning Star had to grasp the side of the sarcophagus to steady her legs. Suddenly, she was looking into a basalt mirror, seeing this reflection and knowing that it was hers. It lasted only a moment.

She was brought back to the present by Snake as he held her elbow and said, "What is it, my wife? Are you ill?"

Morning Star said, "I am quite well, my husband. The shock of the face of the Prophet startled me for a moment. I thought I was looking into a mirror."

She smiled, "I am well. I know what is in the casket. Can we take it up to our quarters? It is late and we can't explore the whole vault tonight, but we can look at the contents of the golden casket before retiring."

Snake said, "Of course."

Eagle carefully lifted the gold casket from the sarcophagus and they left the cavern.

Morning Star turned to Light and said, "You have done well, my Son."

7

The Shaman and the Priestess were training Magnolia and Shell as well as the midwives from the city. Feather was lying on a table in front of them.

Snake said, "I have looked into the body of this woman with the help of Spirit, and I see that she could have problems with her moon and with carrying a child. You may not have this inner vision, but you are still able to help the young women you work with. Many times, it is just a matter of the womb being tilted, or other commonplace problems. Most of these can be helped by a stomach massage that the Priestess will teach you.

"Sometimes, the woman needs certain herbs or plants, and you must know the value of these. Morning Star will teach you about these, also. I will leave you now to your lessons. I ask only that you teach the women you work with about how to do this massage. It will help them if they have pain or bloating during their moon time, and it will give them energy and comfort. Learn it well and teach it. There is no reason that a woman should suffer during this time."

The Shaman left the group of women who were eager to learn all that Morning Star could teach them about these matters.

***

As Snake walked the plaza under the morning sun, he thought about how blessed he had been in life. Events that might have seemed like problems became the way to his happiness.

When he had been taken as a slave, it seemed like a bad thing; but, if it hadn't happened, he would not have met

Deer. When he learned his wife had died, he was very sad, but he had a good life with her and wasn't sorry for that. When the jumping snake had bit him, he was very ill and his spirit had departed. If this hadn't happened, he may never have learned his true calling as a Shaman—and Morning Star may never have realized she loved him.

"Everything is for a reason," he said to himself. He loved his life, and he was able to see that even the darkest moments bring light. That made him think of his son, whom he adored.

The previous evening, after they had all returned from the hidden library, they had brought the golden casket into his and Morning Star's quarters. She had Eagle set it on the table next to the Crystal Skull that her old Priestess had given her. She asked Light to lift the cover, as a reward for finding the treasure. Then she stepped forward and lifted a bundle from the casket. She set it on the table and pulled back the golden cloth which covered it.

It was a second Crystal Skull, seemingly identical to the first. As they all watched, the skulls began to vibrate and glow. Suddenly, a light arched from each of them and met high above the pair. A beautiful tone could be heard, coming from the skulls.

Morning Star turned to her friends and said, "These twin skulls were designed to work together. They will open a doorway for us to step through when we are finished with our work here."

She turned back to the table and began to sing. Suddenly, they could see a bright light growing in size and intensity, forming a doorway between heaven and earth.

Light stood, his eyes shimmering in the glow of the Crystal Skulls, pulled to the doorway as if under a spell— drawn by an overwhelmingly intense desire to walk through. His face glowed as he turned to his mother.

"Do you see it, Nantli? Do you see the light waiting for us on the other side of the door?"

Doorway Series:
Morning Star Rises

With a beautiful smile, he held out his hand to his mother, inviting her to join him. He wanted desperately to walk through, but his strong love for his mother held him back.

"We must wait, my son. It isn't time. The doorway will open for us again—soon, my son. Soon."

She held his hand, unable to let him leave without her. He was so young, not yet beginning his physical changes to manhood. She couldn't let him go yet. She felt his yearning, his disappointment, but she knew the time wasn't right. When it was time, they would all go together.

Works Cited

All references retrieved from the Theosophy Trust, 2006 website:
http://www.theosophytrust.org/tlodocs/articlesTeacher.php
?d=Quetzalcoatl.htm&p=105.

1 Annals of Cuauhtitlan
2 Cantares Mexicanos
3 Cantares Mexicanos
4 Cantares Mexicanos
5,6 Colloquies of the Twelve
7 Codice Matritense